Wicked Gentlemen

Wicked Gentlemen

Ginn Hale

Blind Eye Books
blindeyebooks.com

Wicked Gentlemen
by Ginn Hale

Published by:
Blind Eye Books
1141 Grant Street
Bellingham, Washington 98225
blindeyebooks.com

Edited by Nicole Kimberling.
Cover art and maps by Dawn Kimberling.

This book is a work of fiction and as such all characters and situations are fictitious. Any resemblances to actual people, places or events are coincidental.

First edition October 2007
Copyright © 2007 by Ginn Hale
Printed in the United States of America.

ISBN 978-0-9789861-1-7
Library of Congress Control Number: 2007924792

This book is dedicated to Victor Trevor, because something ought to be.

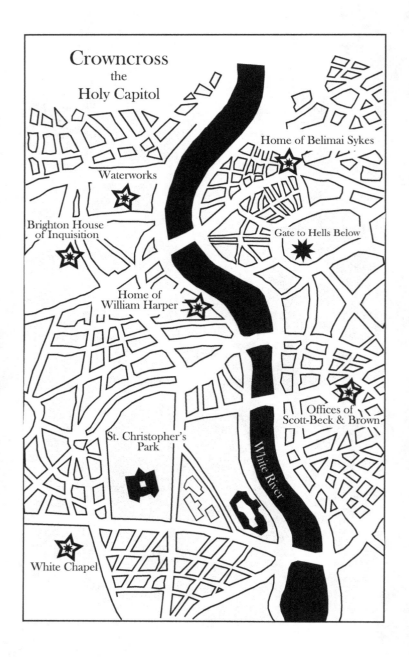

Crowncross
the
Holy Capitol

Home of Belimai Sykes

Waterworks

Brighton House
of Inquisition

Gate to Hells Below

Home of
William Harper

Offices of
Scott-Beck & Brown

St. Christopher's
Park

White River

White Chapel

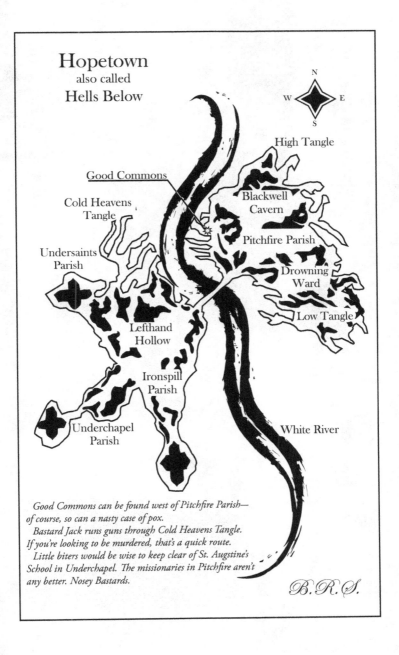

Hopetown
also called
Hells Below

N
W ◆ E
S

High Tangle

Good Commons

Cold Heavens
Tangle

Blackwell
Cavern

Pitchfire Parish

Undersaints
Parish

Drowning
Ward

Low Tangle

Lefthand
Hollow

Ironspill
Parish

Underchapel
Parish

White River

Good Commons can be found west of Pitchfire Parish—
of course, so can a nasty case of pox.
Bastard Jack runs guns through Cold Heavens Tangle.
If you're looking to be murdered, that's a quick route.
Little biters would be wise to keep clear of St. Augstine's
School in Underchapel. The missionaries in Pitchfire aren't
any better. Nosey Bastards.

B.R.S.

∾ Contents ∾

Book One
Mr. Sykes and the Firefly

Book Two
Captain Harper and the Sixty Second Circle

Book One

Mr Sykes and the Firefly

Chapter One
Night

*T*he night hung in tatters. Gas streetlamps chewed at the darkness. Candles cast dull halos through the dirty windows of the tenements across the street. Heavy purple clouds pumped up from smoke stacks and patterned the sky like ugly patches on a black velvet curtain. A few fireflies blinked from what corners of blackness remained.

A pair of them invaded the darkness of my rooms. I watched them flicker, darting through their insectile courtship. They swooped past my face, circled, and then alighted inside the fold of my shirtsleeve.

They crept close to one another, brilliant desire flashing through their tiny bodies. Their antennae touched and quivered. The female firefly reached out and stroked the male. He rushed into her embrace. Holding him close, she crushed her powerful mandibles through his head. Their flickering bodies blinked in perfect unison as she devoured him.

Some romances end more badly than others.

I had to admire the firefly for her neatness. She ate every scrap of evidence and then lounged on my sleeve with an innocent ease that could have fooled an Inquisitor. At last, I flicked her off my arm and rolled up my sleeve. I had my own ruinous affair to cultivate.

Hundreds of small scars cut across the thin muscles of my bare arm. They wound up from my wrists, marking inch after inch of my body with mechanical precision. The scar tissue was as pale as the rest of my skin, but shinier and slightly sunken, like delicate embossing. The scars had faded enough over the years that, given enough darkness or drink, a man might not notice the holy verses carved into my body.

Only the flesh on the inside of my elbow stood out. The white skin and underlying blue veins were buried under a patchwork of bruises and red needle marks. The deep shadows of night could not disguise my ugliness, but beauty was hardly the point. I wanted to be undone, swallowed whole and dissipated into a thoughtless existence. I did not long to be lost in God or Glory; I just wished to be lost.

It hurt when I pushed the needle in through a half-healed scab. But the pain was momentary and it hurt less than going without the ophorium. A feeling like warmth and honey gushed through me. It spilled through my veins, flooded the black chambers of my heart, and slowly burned me away from the inside out. My arms drooped down against the armrests of my chair. The syringe and needle fell to the floor, and I closed my eyes.

For a moment I felt so warm and sweet that I could have been a different person.

I opened my eyes and watched the sky swirling outside my window. Violet ribbons and indigo wind tinted the darkness. Tiny bats swept between black chimneys. Heavy odors of magnolia and rose mingled with the scent of raw sausages. The smell reminded me of the Gold Street whores and those thick perfumes they poured over their sour bodies.

I waited to see what this summer night would bring me.

More often than not, I waited in vain. Still, there were those rare evenings when men came to me. Each had his own kind of desperation. Each had a reason for wanting to draw close to a devil from Hells Below. Some were sweet and sincere; others just couldn't do any worse. It made no difference to me, so long as they could pay.

I wasn't surprised when there was a knock at my door. I drifted from my chair and walked through the room as if I were wading through deep water. A second, far sharper knock followed the first. I didn't hurry. I took in a deep breath, drawing in the scent of my visitor. The smells of birch soap, leather, embalming fluid, and gun oil rushed into my mouth. I paused at the door. The scents entwined but never resolved into a single perfume. After the third knock, I opened the door. Bright light poured in from the hall. I stepped back to evade the sudden illumination. Two men stood in the doorway.

The Inquisition captain caught my attention at once. Just his uniform sent a skittering rush of panic through my languid muscles. A deep desire to slam the door and bolt it shut swept through me. But even when I was drugged to a stupor, my contrary nature arose. I looked the captain over as if he were a mere curiosity. He was a lean man. His black uniform made him seem even more compressed and hard. He wore gloves, as if he did not wish to leave even a fingerprint to attest to where he might have been. His hair was hidden under his cap.

Two silver eyes stared forward from either side of his high black collar, silver emblems of the House of Inquisition. Their harsh metallic gaze burned with reflected light.

The captain's companion was also dressed in the color of his occupation. He wore a white physician's robe and looked nervous. His bare hands clenched together as if offering each other protection from my presence. A gold band gleamed from around one of his fingers—a wedding ring. There was something almost charming about the physician's discomfort. He had the perfect features and strong body of a man who was born with natural beauty. His nervousness made him seem easier to approach; easier to entrap. It made me feel suddenly stronger. If this man had some reason to fear me, then I still had some power, regardless of the Inquisition captain's presence.

"You are Mr. Belimai Sykes?" The captain, in his armor of black cloth and silver emblems, spoke first. He read my name from a tattered business card. The card was almost translucent from age. An edge of the paper cracked off and fluttered to the floor. It looked like a fleck of gold leaf.

I could hardly recall when I had ordered those cards. Had I truly believed that I could slip into good society with nothing more than seventy business cards, a bottle of nail bleach, and a cotton suit? I still had that suit in a drawer in my bedroom. I had been glad to forget which drawer.

I wondered where the captain had come across the card and how long he had been holding it. He carefully placed the card back into a thin silver case and slipped it into his breast pocket. He waited for my response.

"Yes, I'm Belimai Sykes," I said at last. "And you are?"

"William Harper, captain in the Brighton Inquisition." He turned to the physician. "This is my brother in-law, Dr. Edward Talbott."

"How do you do." Dr.Talbott extended his hand. There was a slight alarm in his eyes as he did so. The reflexes of his good breeding had suddenly betrayed him, forcing him to present the bare flesh of his open hand to me.

Dr. Talbott didn't meet my gaze. Perhaps this was the first time that he had come face to face with a living descendant of a demon. Doubtless he had seen amputated limbs and withered cadavers of my kind on his dissection tables. Dr. Talbott had probably even held a Prodigal's tiny black heart in his hands, but a living specimen was a different kind of creature. Clearly, my black nails and dead pallor did not alarm him as much as my hot breath and attentive gaze.

I smiled at Dr. Talbott. His nervousness made me want to come closer. My ancestors once entrapped the souls of men as blonde and succulent as this one.

"Won't you come in?" I asked.

"Yes, of course. Thank you." The physician lowered his hand and stepped into my rooms.

The Inquisition captain paused a moment and then followed his brother in-law inside. I closed the door behind the two of them, locking out the intrusive light of the hall lamps. The two men stood in the darkness of my room. I walked back to my favorite chair and watched the two of them, knowing they couldn't see me well.

"So, what can I do for you gentlemen?" I asked.

"My wife—" Dr. Talbott began, but the captain cut him off.

"I would like your word as to the confidence of this matter." The captain had, of course, dealt with Prodigals before. He knew how to proceed. There was an ancient history of bargains between our two races, and an even longer history of deceptions. Times had changed, but the etiquette remained.

"I have to know what you want me to do before I can swear to do it," I replied.

"We need you to look into a matter for us," the captain replied.

"Just investigation?" It had been a long time since anyone had offered me that kind of work. Years.

I wondered why these two men chose me and how they had found my card. My natural fear of anything linked to the Inquisition weakly roused itself but then was lost a moment later under the pulse of curiosity and ophorium.

"All right." I agreed just to hear what they might say. "You have my word that I will only reveal what I discover to you. So long as I am in your hire."

"I also want your word that you will take no actions without first receiving approval." Captain Harper took a step toward me, but only one.

At this I paused, not because he asked for something odd, but because of what it suggested. He had reason to think that I would take some action. That alone caught my interest. My heart began to beat a little more quickly, a little more deeply. My curiosity opened up like a hungry mouth.

"You have my oath on my name and blood that all I do will be with your consent," I told them, "so long as you agree to the terms of my payment."

"Those listed on your card?" Captain Harper asked.

"Yes." I might have been idealistic when I was younger, but even then I had not offered myself cheaply.

"We agree," Dr. Talbott said. He clearly did not care about money. I guessed that he was the wealthier of the two men. There was something about the scent of his cologne and the fine weave of his suit that assured me that Dr. Talbott could afford my services. The delicate flush of his skin and intensity of his voice hinted that even if he had not had money, Dr. Talbott would have paid me in other ways. I liked that sense of sacrifice and desperation in a client.

"Very well," said the captain. He dropped three gold coins onto the tabletop. It was a small gesture, but binding. Captain Harper did not trust me, which was just as well. I am not a good person. I am naturally inclined to lie. Even my mother had thought so. It was wise of the captain to put his trust in the value of his gold and not in my good faith. Still, I resented him for such insight into my character.

"Come, sit down, and tell me what I can do for the two of you," I said.

They would be clumsy in the dark, but I didn't light a lamp. It was my petty revenge for the hundreds of times bright lights and sunshine had blinded me as I struggled through an appointment in some respectable office.

Dr. Talbott stumbled down onto my old green couch. Captain Harper seated himself in my oak chair. He navigated the room with irritating ease. He must have memorized the furniture arrangement while the light from the hall had illuminated the room. I suppressed my alarm at how observant the man seemed to be.

"A day ago," Dr. Talbott said, "my wife was abducted."

"Certainly the Inquisition is well suited to pursue any criminal matter," I began.

"I would rather not start an official investigation," Captain Harper said. "It is a matter of some delicacy."

"I see." I leaned back in my seat. "If you want my help, it would be best if you were honest with me, even if it does involve a crime." I addressed Dr. Talbott. I liked looking at his wide eyes as he gazed into the shadows, not knowing exactly where I was.

"It's nothing like that." Dr. Talbott clenched his hands together. "No one has done anything wrong. It's just that we want to protect Joan. If anyone were to become aware of her involvements, it could ruin her."

"Involvements?" I prompted.

"Yes." The captain sighed. I could tell from his tone that he disliked revealing information. "My sister has always been inclined toward suffrage for both women and Prodigals. Before she married, Joan was a member of the Good Commons Advocacy

Association. She wrote pamphlets and flyers—nothing of any importance. She left the group five years ago, but she remained in contact with one of the members."

"I see," I said.

"It's quite dark in here, isn't it?" Dr. Talbott said suddenly.

I shrugged, though I doubted that either man could see me well enough to tell. The darkness made me feel so much more powerful than either of them, but I knew I shouldn't add to the physician's discomfort. Not if I wanted him to speak openly to me.

I moved silently from my chair and went to the flint lamp beside Dr. Talbott. He gazed blindly in the direction of my empty seat. With a quick snap of my black nail, I scraped the flint. A tiny spark skipped up into the chamber of the lamp, and the wick burst into flames. Dr. Talbott was almost jolted off the couch.

Captain Harper simply watched me. The pupils of his eyes were still adjusting to the burst of light, so I doubted that he had been able to make out my form in the dark. Somehow he had known where I was. He must have been listening intently. I thought that instead of two eyes emblazoned upon his collar, perhaps Captain Harper should have had an ear. I smiled at the thought.

"You quite startled me." Dr. Talbott laughed nervously.

"I'm sorry, I thought that you'd be more comfortable if there were a little more light." I returned to my seat.

"Oh. Well, thank you. This is better actually." Dr. Talbott glanced around the room. "This is an interesting residence you have. Quite a few books. Do you have a particular area of study?"

Clearly, he hadn't expected that a Prodigal's rooms would contain the same pathetic souvenirs of a life spent in restless solitude that any natural man's might. My shelves overflowed with sheaves of drawing papers, newspaper clippings, broken quills, and stacks of books.

"None at all." I disliked the turn the conversation had taken. "Perhaps you could describe the circumstances of your wife's abduction."

For a moment, Dr. Talbott looked overwhelmed by sorrow. I could taste it. He wanted to talk about anything else.

Dr. Talbott gazed down at his hands mutely. Captain Harper took over.

"Yesterday, Joan and Edward arrived at the Church Banks just a little past two. They went in and set up an investment fund." From Captain Harper's cold tone I would never have thought that he knew either of the people he mentioned. "An acolyte at the Bank recalled that they left the premises less than an hour later. When they reached their carriage, they discovered that someone had used a knife to pry open the door. Joan's silk vanity purse had been stolen. Edward then decided to send Joan home while he walked to the nearest Inquisition House and reported the break in—"

"Mrs. Talbott rode home in the carriage that had been broken into?" I asked.

"Yes," Dr. Talbott said softly. "She insisted that she go immediately and that I report the incident. I was worried about the latch of the door being broken, so I locked it from the outside. Joan had the spare key with her. I thought that she would be fine..." Talbott trailed off and closed his eyes miserably.

Captain Harper leaned forward and patted the other man's shoulder. The gesture did not look quite natural. It seemed like something Captain Harper had seen once in a play and stiffly emulated.

"I'm sorry," Dr. Talbott said. He cleared his throat and sat up straighter. "When I returned home, Thomas, our driver, met me at the gate. He told me that Joan hadn't responded when he called to her. He and the groom, Rollins, thought that she must have fallen ill. They pried the door off, but Joan wasn't inside. She had just vanished from inside the locked carriage."

"Did the driver stop anywhere along the way?" I asked.

"No." Dr. Talbott shook his head. "He took her straight home. It was only a few minutes ride. Our house is just across St. Christopher's Park from the Church Banks. Fifteen minutes at the most."

"Have you received a ransom notice?" I asked. A giddy interest bubbled through me.

"No," Dr. Talbott said. "All we have are the letters from Mr. Roffcale."

"Mr. Roffcale?" The name sounded like a Prodigal's. "He would be the member of Good Commons that your wife kept in contact with?"

"Yes." Dr. Talbott looked surprised that I would guess as much.

"Mr. Roffcale had been sending Joan letters." Dr. Talbott frowned as he said this. "She said they were nothing, just news about her old friends at Good Commons. I never thought anything of them. But after she disappeared, William and I went through them." He seemed unable to go on.

Captain Harper again took up where Talbott left off. "The letters could be seen as incriminating. We discovered warnings that she might be abducted in transport. Another letter described tortures inflicted upon women in graphic detail. Roffcale wanted Joan to return to Good Commons. He claimed that they would protect her."

Harper stood and opened his long black coat. I caught sight of the white priest's collar at his throat as well as the pistol holstered beneath his left arm.

That pairing fit the Inquisition perfectly. The white band proclaimed the captain's authority to judge and redeem the souls of those awash with sin. The pistol embodied the very earthly duty of each man of the Inquisition to enforce and uphold the law. Salvation became far more appealing when damnation was faced at gunpoint.

Captain Harper withdrew a bundle of letters from the inner pocket of his coat and handed them to me. His leather gloves brushed against my fingers, and I felt the slight sting of the holy oils used to cure the hide.

Captain Harper was close enough that I could see his eyes and smell his breath. His eyes were dark brown with deep blue shadows beneath them. His breath was nothing but tobacco smoke and coffee. I guessed that he had not eaten recently, nor had he slept.

"These are the letters." Captain Harper stepped back from me before I could catch a deeper impression of him.

"Do you have any idea where Mr. Roffcale might be now?" I turned the bundle of letters over, checking the postmarks and return addresses. All of the letters came from Hells Below.

"He's in custody at the Brighton Inquisition House," Captain Harper said.

I frowned at the thought. It was an unpleasant place to be for anyone, but the worst tortures were reserved for Prodigals. The prayer engines were a particular horror. The scars on my chest and arms burned from just the memory.

"I'm not sure what you could need me for, then. If he's in your power already, I'm sure you'll be able to extract all the information you'd like to have."

"Right now, I'm just holding him. If I have him taken in for a confession, then everything he says goes down in the confessor's records. I would rather not have his name mixed with Joan's if it can be helped," Captain Harper said.

"If it can't be helped?" I asked.

"We will do anything that is required to see that Joan is returned unharmed." Dr. Talbott's low voice trembled with conviction.

Captain Harper gazed out the open window behind me. He studied the empty blackness for several moments and then turned his attention back to me.

"All we want is for you to go in and talk with Roffcale. He's more likely to relax with one of his own. Hopefully, he'll let something slip to you that he wouldn't tell me."

"You're paying quite a bit, just to have me chat a man up," I replied.

"I'm sure I can find more for you to do if that isn't enough," the captain replied.

I glanced up at him. I had no doubt that there was more he would have me do. I glanced out the window. Pairs of fireflies flashed and chased each other across the darkness.

"I suppose that you'll want me to go to the Inquisition House to speak to this Roffcale?" I knew that would be the case but still asked, hoping that somehow I'd be wrong.

"Tonight would be best." Captain Harper buttoned up his coat.

"Yes, I suppose it would," I said.

"Thank you so much." Dr. Talbott stood quickly.

I nodded and picked my coat up off the back of my chair. As I pulled it on, I remembered my fallen hypodermic. I glanced down quickly, wondering if the captain might have caught sight of it. Fortunately, it had rolled under my chair. The only thing on the floor that the captain might have seen was a single, tattered insect wing.

Chapter Two
Silver

*D*r. Talbott had a patient who needed his attention and so parted company with Captain Harper and me at Baker Station. Captain Harper and I rode the carriage in silence to the Brighton House of Inquisition.

The big stone building was clean and furiously lit. The doors separating the long halls were etched with blazing silver eyes. Pairs of eyes glared from the walls and stared down from the ceiling. Lime lamps were lit inside them so that the pupils shone like searchlights. Every reflective surface caught the light and ignited to white fire. I flinched from the searing illumination but couldn't find a dim corner or dark shadow. Silver light slashed through my thin eyelids. I held my hand up to shade my eyes. From beneath the shadow of my hand, I stole glances around.

The bare intensity of the light burned the color out of everything. Beside me, Captain Harper's black form looked like a moth-gray shadow. His face was like a ghost's: so white that I could hardly distinguish one feature from another. Only the deep shadow that his cap cast over his eyes remained. It lay over his features like a velvet mask.

"The silver must be burning you quite a bit now," he said as we walked through another set of doors. His tone was neither pleased nor sorry. He said it as if it was simply something to talk about as we walked.

"Yes," I replied. "This particular House seems very well-designed to that purpose."

"The light makes it easier to control Prodigal offenders. Turn right here. There's only a little farther to go." He turned and I dimly stumbled after him. I could imagine the power Captain Harper felt, having me so completely helpless. I decided that no matter what we discovered from Roffcale, I would make it my business to take the captain with me to Hells Below. I would find some reason that we would need to descend into that wet blackness and see how the man fared out of his element.

Murky, gray tears filled my eyes. The light stung and seared every inch of my uncovered body. The tops of my hands turned pink. This was not the first time I had been in a House of Inquisition, and this was far from the worst pain I had endured in such a place. This was only the malevolent gaze. It was a look that could sear and blind, but alone, it could not kill.

Death came by slow degrees on the hard metal tables of the Confessional rooms. It was done with simple questions and endless patience. Unlike the depictions in protest flyers, the Houses of Inquisition did not flow with rivers of blood. The walls were not stained with gore or hung with rusted hooks. The Houses were holy places. They were quiet, clean, and bright. Even the Confessional rooms were subdued and calm. The Inquisitors and Confessors never taunted or screamed threats. They asked politely for everything. The silver knives, nails, and prayer engines were merely devices with which they sought absolute truth. All they demanded was complete honesty.

That was the true horror of the Inquisition's inner chambers. It was there in every pair of those unwavering eyes. The Inquisition would expose every inch of you. They discovered every function and flaw of your naked, shaking body. They dug every fear and shame out of its safe darkness. Sweet, private secrets and half-forgotten crimes, even those petty lies of vanity—none of them could be hidden. The Confessors extracted desire and illusion like rotten teeth.

And then perhaps you would die.

Some confessions were easier to make than others.

"Here." Harper stopped. "We just put him in a holding cell."

Captain Harper unlocked a door and we stepped into a cool dimness. The lime lamps in the room had been lowered. Someone had misted the room with rosewater. The humidity eased my burning skin, but the perfume only partially disguised the smell of urine and blood emanating from Roffcale's corpse. Harper stared at the body in shock. I turned away, preferring the blinding lime light to the gutted remains that lay in the shadows.

Chapter Three
Red Ale

*A*fter discovering a handsome young man with his bowels cut out and his genitals sliced like sandwich meat, I had no desire to remain in the Inquisition House. I closed my eyes and waited while Harper reported the murder and checked the visitor ledger for entries. No one unusual had come to see Roffcale before Harper and me. Far down the hall, I heard Harper's muted exchange with an acolyte. I only caught the last few words: "Well, he didn't do it to himself, damn it. Someone had to have gone in to see him."

The smell of Roffcale's mutilated body drifted over me. The fecal reek of spilled intestines and the sharp odor of blood churned under a cloud of rose perfume. Nausea bubbled up through my stomach as acolytes carried buckets of Roffcale's remains past me. Acolytes wrapped larger sections of his body in cloths and carried them out like newborn infants.

"Captain." I caught Harper as he strode back toward the cell. "There doesn't seem to be much sense in my remaining to talk to Mr. Roffcale at this point."

"No." Captain Harper scowled. "Let's get out of here, before you start to blister."

"That would be good."

I followed Captain Harper through the halls and back out into the night.

"Come on." He beckoned me down the street. "I owe you a drink after all of this."

The idea of gin appealed to me. I certainly wasn't going to turn in for a night's sleep with the memory of Roffcale's corpse so fresh in my mind. I followed Captain Harper.

He led the way through the narrow streets and cut across alleys, moving more like a cutpurse than a captain of the Inquisition. I followed him, pleased that we were sinking into an environment that suited me.

The roads were muddy and piled with trash. Puddles of filthy water pooled over the walkways and mixed with the heavy smell of horse shit that permeated the streets. None of the buildings were well-marked. Harper turned to a squat heap of soot-stained bricks and disappeared down a flight of steps. As I descended after him, I noticed a faded painting on the right wall of the stairs. It looked like the head of a growling mastiff. The door at the bottom of the stairs was painted with the same dog. A circle of flames wreathed its neck like a collar.

I followed Captain Harper into the heavy scent of cigar smoke, spilled beer, and sweat. Inside, the breath and bodies of the men packed into the rooms filled the air with hot animal odors. Warm condensation dampened the walls. The rumble of voices rose and dropped through a constant murmur. The men's faces were thick and awkward, like the dried remains of mudslides. They hardly glanced up when Captain Harper came in. I only received one fat splatter of spit hacked at my feet. Captain Harper chose a table in the back.

We sat drinking in silence for some time. The easy collapse into an alcoholic haze made relations between Captain Harper and me simple. It became a matter of proximity. We were there together, but we were not there for each other. We were there for the drinks. It was the same with every other man in the cramped bar. In a way, it was deeply pleasant to share the sense that in this place no one wanted your concern or tactful conversation. It was a lazy community of mutual disinterest and alcohol.

Captain Harper drained a pint of red ale and immediately started on a second. He drooped forward slightly, leaning his forehead on one of his gloved hands while he studied the contents of his glass.

"It would be easy to get out of a carriage if you had the key," he said.

I didn't reply. I wasn't even sure he was talking to me.

I gulped back a shot of blue gin and quickly poured myself another from the bottle.

"If she unlocked the door on the far side, while Edward was locking the other, she could have slipped out before the driver pulled away." Harper turned toward me. At some point he had pulled his cap down even farther over his face. I could only see his mouth.

"But this with Roffcale... " Harper shook his head.

I wasn't sure if it was the third shot of gin or my self-destructive nature, but I was suddenly very interested in getting that damn hat off of Harper's head. I leaned in a little closer.

"I don't want you to tell Edward about Roffcale, all right?" Harper told me.

"No?" I lowered my head so that I could peer in under the brim of Harper's cap. His brown eyes were almost closed.

"I paid you and I made you give me your word. You're in my hire, not his."

"So that's how it is," I said.

"Yes, that's how it is." He sighed, then closed his eyes. For a moment I thought he might pass out, but he pulled himself back upright. "We're going to have to look into some filthy places, and I don't want Edward getting mixed up in it."

"It's your money," I said.

"What are you doing with my hat?" Captain Harper demanded as he felt my fingers slide up and grab hold of it.

"Trying it on," I replied. Then I whipped it off him and slapped it crookedly onto my own head.

"So, do I look like a captain in the Inquisition?"

"Not by half." Captain Harper smiled. His hair was a little longer than I had expected, and lighter in color. "Those black claws of yours would give you away in a breath."

"Not if I had a pair of gloves." I glanced down at Captain Harper's gloved hands.

He laughed at that and then finished his ale in one long drink. I poured myself another shot of gin but didn't drink. I held the shot glass up and watched the way the liquid distorted the image of Captain Harper's face. There was something fascinating about the way it flawed his features. It only took a tiny shift, just a curve of glass, to ruin him.

"So," I said, still watching Captain Harper through the shot glass, "you think your sister just got out of the carriage herself?"

"I thought so, but..." Captain Harper broke off and stared at his gloved hands. "But finding Roffcale like that...I don't know, now."

"Why were you holding Roffcale if you didn't think he abducted your sister?"

"I thought she had run off with him." Captain Harper picked up my gin bottle and turned it slowly in his hands. "They were lovers when they were in Good Commons. Edward never knew about that. I wanted to save him from finding out." Captain Harper shook his head. "I figured that if I took Roffcale in, Joan would show up on her own."

"That doesn't seem to have been the case." I held my full shot glass out to Captain Harper.

Captain Harper stared at the glass in my hand, then took it. They say that blue gin can strip paint. He swallowed it like medicine. Then he poured out another shot and pushed the glass over to me. Briefly, the memory of Roffcale's delicate features and the filthy chasm of his belly came to my mind. I took my shot of gin and shoved the glass back to Captain Harper. He filled it slowly, with deliberate care.

"What was done to him was exactly what he'd written about to Joan. I think he really was trying to warn her." He closed his eyes. "God only knows what's happened to her."

"Drink up," I said.

Captain Harper frowned at the glass. "I don't usually drink the hard stuff, you know."

"It gets easier as you go," I assured him.

"I know," Captain Harper replied. "That's why I don't do it often. It gets too easy."

"I'd be the last man to criticize." I warmed to Captain Harper slightly at the thought that he had spent nights swilling drunk on blue gin.

"I suppose so," he replied.

Captain Harper tossed the shot back. Then he rolled the empty shot glass across the table to me.

"I think I might have gotten the wrong impression of you when we first met." I filled the shot glass.

"Oh?" Captain Harper asked.

"I expected that you'd be stiffer," I said.

Captain Harper smirked at my choice of words.

"Mr. Sykes." Captain Harper leaned in closer to me. I could smell the thick scent of ale on his lips. "Don't be taken in by a priest's collar. We in the Inquisition dance with devils more often than most whores in Hells Below."

"Well, if I ever need a partner, perhaps I should look you up, Captain Harper." I swallowed my shot and placed the glass in Harper's gloved hand. He filled the glass, drank, then poured another and placed it in front of me.

"We're already partners of a kind, aren't we, Mr. Sykes?" he asked.

"Of a kind," I agreed.

"Of a kind," he repeated, as if there were some other meaning in the words.

I matched him and he downed another. Steadily, we made our way through the entire bottle. We gave ourselves up to the act of going on. We drank shot after shot of searing gin. Sinking down into drunkenness, the constant rhythm of passing the glass and drinking became our purpose.

When you drink like that, it isn't for pleasure. It's because your thoughts have become diseases. You do it because it's the only easy cure you can find.

Captain Harper moved slowly and carefully, as if his body had become a mechanism that required all his concentration to navigate through the bar. His eyes were hardly open. He leaned against me and moved with my steps as I steadily lead him out of the dark solace of the bar and up into the city streets. The night was wearing thin. I could feel the golden light of the rising sun streaking the horizon with its heat.

Behind us the bar owner peered out between his doors, pretending that he was locking up. He watched to see what business there could be between a Prodigal like me and a man of the Inquisition.

"You know, Captain," I whispered, "staggering drunk down the street with me can't do much for your reputation."

"Fuck 'em," Captain Harper slurred softly into my ear, then pulled his cap off of my head.

I let him have it back. His breath brushed against the back of my neck. His lips just touched my skin for a moment as he sagged into me. It had been months since I had taken a lover, even for a night. It had been too long, I realized. I sank back into my temptations. Captain Harper didn't seem to care, and at the moment neither did I. By my nature, I am a creature caught in the grip of my desires. At times they make me unwise, but it has never been in me to deny them.

I led Captain Harper back to my rooms and peeled off his black coat and his priest's collar. Slowly, I worked his gloves off, exposing his long fingers. His nails were as pink and glossy as the insides of a seashell. Each was tipped with a perfect white crescent. I kissed the soft skin of his palm. His stainless body was everything my own would never be. I hungered for that perfection.

I slipped Captain Harper's pistol out of its holster and had all that I wanted of Harper that night. I did not worry over the next morning or the lies we muttered as our bodies twined together. For one evening, the gin had cured us of our thoughts—that was enough.

Chapter Four
Old Ink

*R*offcale's letters smelled of dried blood and very cheap cologne. I pulled in his scent while my fingertips brushed over the clumsy lines of his reform school script. He was young and passionate. He poured himself into each word with absurd intensity. With every letter he set down, he fell in love and was overwhelmed with rage. His odes to Joan Talbott's beauty were terrible. Roffcale stacked cliché upon cliché until they achieved a staggering tower of artless adoration. Roffcale's miserable poetry acquired poignancy with its absolute conviction. He meant every word.

Roffcale's desperate warnings to Joan were just that: attempts to protect a woman he could not even approach in public. Joan Talbott was from good society and Peter Roffcale was an underage con man with nails as black as any demon's.

I leafed through the pages of his letters, touching the paper where Joan's hands had moved over Roffcale's words.

Roffcale had pressed his palms into the pages to hold them still as he wrote. He had run his fingers under difficult words, checking his spelling. Joan had carefully pulled pages close to hide the contents from anyone else. I felt the faded places where she had run her fingers over his words again and again. Every piece of paper had carried his touch to her. Many of his letters were stained with a pale pink tint where Joan had pressed her lips to his closing signature.

The sweetness of them both made me sick and slightly jealous. I searched ahead to the details that Harper had mentioned. Roffcale was more skilled at writing about murder than he was at love poetry. He was familiar with the sight of beaten corpses of whores and cum beggars. He described the bodies in the same simple way that he might have given directions to a bakery.

Her belly was slashed under the ribs and then down to her crotch. That was a mess. All sliced up and the inside pulled out. Lots of pieces of her were missing. Her guts were all spilled out of her. The bastard who did it rooted through her insides like he was looking for hidden treasure. Rose was the third one and I don't want to see it done again. It was ugly work just looking at it. Come back.

I'm begging now. Please come back.

Roffcale had described the condition in which Harper and I had found his own body quite well. I felt a slight coldness seep up from the page of Roffcale's letter. It had the sharp sting of premonition. Roffcale had feared he would die this way; perhaps he had even known it. I turned back to the first page of the letter.

Roffcale had scrawled a few lines in the margin. I had mistaken them for poetic gibberish at first glance. Now I realized that he had written them in the only empty space there was left after the letter had been finished. The writing was worse than usual.

I had a dream
that I was the fourth one
laying there
with Lily and Rose
all cut apart
Come Now.

It struck me as odd that he would constantly ask her to come to Hells Below. The murders seemed to have been taking place there or close by. Why would he want Joan Talbott to come there for protection when she would have been far safer in her husband's home? If Roffcale knew he could not save his own life, what protection did he think he could offer Joan, I wondered. I frowned and gazed at the lines of old ink.

I'm begging. Please come back.

It hardly sounded like a promise of protection. In fact, it seemed like the opposite. Suddenly, a thought came to me. What if Peter Roffcale had not been offering his protection, but begging for hers? I glanced at the date on the letter. It was quite recent, only a day before Joan Talbott had disappeared. I folded the pages back into a bundle and slid them into their rough pulp envelope. The postmark on the envelope showed that it had gone out the next morning. Joan Talbott would have read it only a few hours before she vanished.

"So?" Harper's voice caught me off guard. I almost jumped, he was so close behind me.

"So, what?" I replied as coldly as I could. I turned back to him slowly.

Harper had located his clothes and dressed. Only his cap was missing. I caught his puzzled glance toward my hat rack. I smiled at that. The night before I had stuffed his cap into one of the spider-infested filing cases under my bed.

Harper's hair tangled around his face like a thorn briar. His eyes were red, rimmed, and bloodshot from the excesses of the evening before. Without a cap shadowing his features, his exhaustion and youth were easy to see. He seemed vulnerable despite the hard black lines of his Inquisitor's coat. That almost made up for him surprising me.

"What do you think?" he asked.

"I think that we need to go to Roffcale's residence at Good Commons." I stood up, grabbed my coat and smoked-glass spectacles, then glanced back at Harper. "Are you hungry?"

"Not right now," he replied.

"Badly hung-over?" Perhaps I sounded a little too pleased, but Harper didn't seem to care. Perhaps taunting was what he expected of my kind, even after a night spent together.

"No." Harper pushed his fingers through his wild hair. "I just haven't had much of an appetite lately."

Of course not. His sister was missing and quite possibly dead. It was no wonder that I had been able to get him so drunk, so easily. He probably hadn't eaten in days.

"It'll only get worse if you don't eat something." I reluctantly found myself picking up my own black wool cap and tossing it to Harper. "We'll stop in at Mig's. They have decent beef pies there."

Harper turned the cap over in his hands and then put it on. It fit about as well as his old one had, though this cap was more scuffed. It smelled lightly of my hair. I wondered if Harper noticed.

"Before we go..." Harper adjusted the cap so that his eyes were once again shadowed.

"Yes?" I was already at the door with one hand wrapped around the knob.

"About last night..." Harper shifted slightly. "I think it would be best if we got it clear between the two of us—"

"I have no intention of telling anyone, if that's what you're worried about." I smiled so that Harper could see my long teeth. "And I don't think you're likely to be bragging about it, so what's left to say?"

"No, I meant between us...We were both pretty drunk. I just wanted you to understand that..." Harper paused, unwilling to go on. Steadily, the pause began to spread into a lingering silence. He seemed unable to make himself speak of the night before. It amused, but didn't surprise me.

"You wanted to make it clear that it was just a drunk fuck?" I filled in for him at last.

"I'm not sure those are the words I would have used," Harper replied.

"It was a good tumble, Captain. But rest assured, I haven't fallen madly in love with you. Just forget about it, and let's get on with our business." I turned the knob experimentally, feeling the latch slide free and then slip back. Discussions after sex always ran the chance of turning ugly. Or worse, sentimental. I pulled the door open just a crack.

"I just wanted to make sure we were of the same mind," Harper said at last.

"Well, I've told you what I think. So, are we agreed?" I asked.

"Yes," Harper said.

"Then that's all there is to say about it," I said.

Harper nodded and I opened the door with a sense of relief.

It was pleasant to find another man as willing to let go as myself. Others had lingered in my bed and concerned themselves with the syringes scattered across my desk. They had clung to me as I descended into ruin. Some had attempted to save me. I had been wept on, slapped, and pulled into a dozen chapels by men who had mistaken me for their true love.

None of them had understood that my moments of sweetness were pure ophorium. Everything that they seemed to love about me came from the needles they detested. The man they desired was an illusion, an ugly stone made briefly beautiful by a trick of the light. In their own ways, each of them had fallen as deeply in love with my addiction as I had. None of them had known how absurd they were, begging me to leave behind the drug that was the source of all they loved most about me. My kindness, my calm, even my careless ease. Ophorium made me their perfect lover because it erased the truth of what I was.

When it coursed through my body, I burned free of thought and memory. That radiant absolution was far more consuming than any number of desperate climaxes against another man's sweating flesh.

I doubted that Harper concerned himself with any of this, but at least he didn't care. We descended into the evening with a comfortable distance between us.

Chapter Five
Ghosts

*T*he sun sat back against the horizon like a bloated foreman refusing to end the day. It poured its yellow heat across the city streets, baking the horse shit and mud into a steaming soup. Flies, dogs, and filthy children zipped through the hot muck while horse carriages and wagons stirred it into a seeping river. It stank in a way that fans and perfume-soaked kerchiefs couldn't begin to disguise. The radiant sunlight only made things seem worse. It illuminated each fetid detail of day around me. The bare ugliness of everything under the sun repulsed me.

I strode toward the staircase ahead. A massive granite arch rose up over the wide stone steps, which lead down into humid blackness. It was one of the thirteen gateways that lead down into the Prodigal ghetto. The actual gates had been removed, but the engraving in the archway remained: *They who were lost shall be found.*

I imagined that the men who wrote those words had higher aspirations than most of us who passed beneath them into the city below.

Some optimistic bishop had christened the place Hopetown. Anyone who had ever gone there called it Hells Below. That summed it up well enough.

It might have been beautiful three hundred years ago when the Covenant of Redemption had brought my fallen ancestors up from Damnation. They abandoned their great kingdom of endless darkness in exchange for the promise of Salvation for themselves and their descendants.

The walls of the staircase were adorned with mosaics of the Great Conversion. Ashmedai, Sariel, Satanel. The pride and glory of hell had come in their robes of fire, in their chariots of beaten gold. Some were adorned with jewels, while others wore the polished bones of the angels that had fallen beneath their blades. They had each bowed down before the Silver Cross and submitted to baptism at the hands of the Inquisition.

The brilliant glazes were darkened with lamp smoke and factory grease now, but the images were still discernable. Somewhere among the glittering host of demons, one of my own ancestors stood. They all looked fierce and beautiful. I found it difficult to imagine that I could have descended from such creatures.

The blood had certainly thinned.

The carved temples and catacombs that had once been a city of hope had decayed into dank ghetto. Hundreds of tunnels riddled Hells Below now. City sewer pipes and massive gas lines invaded every space and dripped with condensation. The lattice of temple walls had collapsed. Now, vast caverns gaped wide with tenement houses and ore sluices. The children of hell's greatest lords had been bred down into coal miners.

Relegated by law to the confines of the capital city, few Prodigals even attempted to leave Hells Below. They stayed down where they at least had each other for company, as well as the comfort of cavernous darkness. Only the worst of our kind lived in the city above. Criminals, exiles, and addicts. I supposed I fit all three descriptions at one time or another.

"Did you want me to carry this beef pie around for some purpose?" Harper asked.

"I thought you might want to eat it," I replied, though in truth I had just wanted to get rid of it.

"One was more than enough." Harper suddenly turned and rushed back up several of the steps. He stopped in front of a woman who had been working her way up the stairs and handed her the pie. Then he strode back down beside me.

"Well, that takes care of that," he said.

"Was she a Prodigal?" I glanced back quickly at the woman, but the sun from above burned out most of my vision. All I had noticed as she passed me on the steps had been the numerous lace shawls that hung over her back and arms. She moved slowly, as if she were either extremely old or extremely drunk.

"Bright yellow eyes and fingernails blacker than yours," Harper commented. "I couldn't see her ears, but I don't doubt they were pointed. Her teeth sure as hell were. She hissed at me too." He seemed amused by this.

"She probably thought you were handing her poison." I looked meaningfully at the silver eyes of the Inquisition that glinted from either side of Harper's collar.

"Not every man joins the Inquisition just to burn Prodigals. We uphold the law as well," Harper said as we continued down the stairs. "Sooner or later, some of you are bound to figure that out."

"I wouldn't bet my bread money on that." I had to glance away to suppress the flare of anger that rushed through me. I knew quite well how the men of the Inquisition dealt with Prodigals. I had been burned once myself, but that was long past and none of Harper's business.

"We are a surprisingly stubborn bunch," I said.

"So you are." Harper smiled.

We stepped down into the heavy darkness of Hells Below. The warm air hung over us in swathes. The thick flavors of so many Prodigals living so close saturated every breath with a taste like a heavy chemical perfume. The scents rolled into each other, smelling by turns of violets, sulfur, urine, and fragrant lamps. It wasn't easy to take in. Each breath was like a long drag from a cigarette. I had forgotten how familiar its taste was.

Harper coughed and had to take several slow breaths before he adjusted to the air.

As we walked, I noticed the skin on his exposed cheeks began to take on a pink flush as though it was sunburned. His eyes seemed irritated also. Harper just pulled his cap a little lower and continued moving as if it was no trouble to him at all. In fact, he seemed as familiar with the place as he had been with the bars of Brighton.

He strode through the narrow streets with the natural ease of a man who had been here before. He took alley shortcuts without glancing up to check a street name or number.

"Do you come here often?" I asked as we trudged down a narrow side road. The gaslight of the streetlamps flickered. Drops of condensed breath, sweat, and steam spattered down on us from the cavern ceiling far above.

"Have I surprised you?" Harper glanced sidelong at me.

"No." I didn't like the smugness of his tone. "I just thought that you would be more acquainted with Brighton than Hells Below."

"I did my first three years of foot patrol down here." Harper stepped onto a walkway of planks. I followed him. Oily liquid lapped up from just below the wooden boards as we walked over them.

"Did you make many Prodigal friends while you were here?" I asked, knowing that he couldn't have.

"Of course not." Harper looked back at me. "Did you ask just to hear me say so?"

"That could very well be the case." I grinned, showing Harper my long white teeth.

"You really are quite unique, aren't you, Mr. Sykes?" he said.

Harper's words satisfied me strangely. If he had complimented my wild black hair or my butter-colored eyes, I would have thought he was mocking me and hated him for it. If he had called me twisted or perverse, I would have secretly thought of jabbing him in the eye. But somehow he had known just the right words to give me a burst of warmth. I glanced ahead to the street number on one of the gray shale houses, deliberately ignoring Harper so that he would not know how his words pleased me.

"That's the one." I pointed to the hulking blue building just ahead of us.

"So it is," Harper replied.

The woman who answered the door looked at Harper intently for several moments before she let us in. She was tall, pale, and waxy. There was a transparency to her skin. The lamplight in the house seemed to glow through her. The shadows she cast were faint.

She walked us down a narrow hall and into a large, windowless waiting room in absolute silence. Her pale yellow dress didn't even rustle as she walked.

The waiting room seemed like it had been nice a long time ago. The chair I sat in rocked on its uneven legs. A dust of incense ash rose up from the upholstered arms. Harper seated himself on the high-backed settee across from me. Its red upholstery was dappled with faded shades of pink and brown. Dozens of mismatched candles covered the heavy wooden table in the middle of the room. Dried spills of wax drooped over the edge of the tabletop and clung to the carved legs.

There was a deeply familiar scent in the air. Something like mulled wine. I had smelled it before, a long time ago. I took a deep breath and held the taste in my mouth. It was smoky and warm. Tiny tongues of scent and heat caressed the insides if my mouth. It tasted like demonic conjuring. Uneasiness seeped through my muscles.

The woman who had shown us in pulled the door closed. She flipped the lock and stared at Harper, her waxen features melting into an expression of rage.

"So, Captain, have you brought this man in exchange for Roffcale?" She waved her hand at me. "Did you think that's all it would take for you to walk back in here and get out alive?"

"This is Belimai Sykes." Harper's eyes were once again hidden. His mouth was as expressionless as a gash. "He's a private consultant whom I have hired to investigate the circumstances of Joan's disappearance."

"And what about Peter, you bastard?" She raised her thin white hands. Her black nails glittered in the lamplight like chips of flint. "You said you'd have him back by morning. You said he'd be fine."

"I'm sorry about Roffcale, Mica." Harper's voice was flat, the same way it had been when he had first hired me. "There's an internal inquiry going on right now. We'll find out what happened and the guilty party will be punished."

"What? Is that another of your promises, Captain?" she snapped.

"I can't give you more than my word, Mica." Harper leaned forward, his elbows resting on his knees. He steepled his gloved fingers beneath his mouth. "You know as well as I do that I didn't kill Roffcale."

"How do I know that?" Mica demanded.

"I wouldn't be here if I had." Harper let out a tired sigh. "Mica, someone got to Roffcale in prison, and the same person took Joan. I have to find out who it was. I need help to do that."

"I should tear you to pieces," Mica said.

"Help us find Roffcale's murderer," Harper said quietly. "Then you can rip me into as many shreds as you like."

"I just might, Harper." Mica glared at him, then glanced away. "So, what do you want? More of our people to sacrifice for your sister's sake?"

Harper didn't respond to the accusation. He simply answered her first question as if she hadn't said anything else.

"I just need to talk to Nick," Harper said.

"You honestly think he'll do anything for you, after this?" Mica asked.

"I'm the lesser of two evils. If he doesn't help me, then he ensures that these killings go on."

"You're a heartless bastard, Harper."

Harper said nothing. At last Mica turned the lock and opened the door.

"I'll get him." She left the room.

"You take me to the nicest places," I whispered to Harper.

"You're the one who decided we should come here." Harper leaned back into the padding of the settee.

"You might have mentioned that all the members of Good Commons were going to want to kill you before we walked in."

"What's life without a few surprises?" Harper flashed his hand up at me. "Don't answer that. It was a rhetorical question."

"Are you still drunk from last night?" I asked.

"No." Harper smiled. "Having my life threatened always makes me a little giddy."

"Giddy?"

"I have to find my pleasures where I can."

"I'd be hesitant to call that exchange with Mica pleasant." I scraped at a droplet of wax on the arm of my chair.

"You ought to allow a man to retain his conceits, Mr. Sykes."

The slight smile on Harper's lips sank back to a flat line. "It wasn't pleasant. It shouldn't have been. I gave her my word that Roffcale would be safe in my care...He should have been safe."

"Yes, he should have been."

Both Harper and I looked up at the man who stepped through the doorway. I stared at him for several moments longer than his sudden entry deserved. It was strange to be startled, not by his silent appearance, but by the familiarity of his face and voice. He, too, seemed taken off guard by the sight of me.

I should have known from the moment I tasted the air in the room. The scent of conjuring melted with the musk of his sweat and the camphor oil he rubbed into his skin to give it a golden sheen. It was the singular essence of Nickolas Sariel.

He had hardly changed, despite the years. His eyes were still the color of opium poppies. His hair was like fire, winding through streaks of smoky red, yellow, and white. His black nails had grown longer, but they still gleamed with the same carefully filed edges.

I saw him take in a quick breath of the air as he stared at me. He would have expected to smell fresh ink and the must of old books lingering on me. But I was no longer the man he had known, and the scents of my body had become far more bitter.

"Belimai?" He whispered my name as he came closer.

There was an instant when I wanted to say yes. But a stinging pain flared through the prayers engraved into my skin.

"No." I glanced down at the wax spattered arm of my chair. "I'm afraid you've mistaken me for someone else. I'm sorry."

That was all I had to say. Sariel would not allow himself to ask a second time. He immediately turned to Harper.

"So, Captain, Mica tells me you want my help."

Harper paused for a moment, looking between Sariel and myself. We said nothing. Harper shook his head and pressed on.

"I need you to reach Joan if you can."

"Are you asking me to use my powers as the presiding officer of Good Commons? Or were you thinking of something less in keeping with the law?" Sariel crossed his arms over his chest.

"Because if it's the latter, I want you to understand that the price runs very high. I won't work for free, not for you."

"You're not the first devil I've dealt with." Harper gestured to me but Sariel didn't look. "I'm aware of the going rates." Harper reached into his jacket and dropped several gold coins into Sariel's hand.

I couldn't help but wonder where Harper was coming up with all the money. Perhaps Talbott was financing him. That, or he was bankrupting himself. It bothered me that I didn't know his nature well enough to decide if he would use another man's money or only his own.

Sariel studied the coins in his hand, then shook his head. "I was thinking of a little more, Captain Harper."

Harper handed Sariel more fistfuls of coins. Harper went through every one of the pockets of his coat and even gave Sariel his watch and chain. He did it in a matter of a fact manner. If there was any expression on his face, it might have been that look of slight amusement that seemed to pass over his lips at the strangest times.

"That's all I have," Harper said at last. "If you want more, you'll have to wait until I'm paid at the end of the month."

"All I wanted was everything you had." Sariel piled the coins on the table without even counting them. I counted them. He had taken almost ten times what Harper had paid me.

"I'll hold the summons here." Sariel pushed the door shut.

He walked around the table twice, moving the candles until they formed a series of circles within each other. He whispered softly to himself as he walked. I recognized some of the words from the curses he used to spit out behind teachers' backs at St. Augustine's reform school.

"...Ashmedai, your flame." He swept his hands over the outer ring of candles and the wicks lit up. The flames skipped like stones across water, lighting circle after circle of candles. "Sariel, father of my bloodline, your power..." Sariel went on.

The flames of the candles began to burst up into geysers of fire. Sariel continued circling. His eyes were open but not focused.

He whispered words so quickly that I could hardly catch more than hisses of his breath. Each time Sariel let out another string of incantations, the flames surged up, forming a rolling mass of blazing fire.

I couldn't help but glance at Harper. He sat still, watching Sariel with his fingers steepled and pressed against his lips.

"Lucifer, light bearer, lord of wisdom." Sariel came to a stop only a few steps in front of me. He raised his arms, then slashed the long talons of his left hand across the open palm of his right hand. A deep furrow of blood gushed up. Sariel thrust his bleeding palm into the fire. A scent of searing camphor choked the air.

"Show me this woman," he hissed as the tongue of fire surged up over his hand. "My will is greater than even your own." Sariel grasped a single flame and lifted it up above the rest.

"Show me," he commanded.

Suddenly the candles dimmed to mere sparks. The single flame in Sariel's hand leapt up to a blinding white heat. It twisted and rolled, growing larger and brighter. Slowly it formed the soft curves of a woman. Smoke rolled and wound over her, adding shadows and dark hollows to her luminous flesh. She floated above Sariel's outstretched arm, gazing out at the empty corner of the room.

"Joan." Harper came to his feet and stepped up to the edge of the table.

As the woman turned I studied her face. She was beautiful. Her dark eyes were wide and luminous. Her black hair had been pulled down and hung in long curls around her torn clothes. Her mouth moved, but only a curl of white smoke poured out. She looked frightened.

"Is she alive?" Harper demanded.

Sariel said nothing. His eyes were clenched shut as he concentrated. Tremors of strain passed through his arm. Slowly he nodded his head in answer to Harper.

"Where is she?" Harper asked.

"There's a man...a Prodigal..." Sariel pushed the words out between tight gasps of air. "He's dead...like the others...There's blood and broken glass everywhere...Someone else..."

Suddenly I felt the air change. An acrid bitter scent, like scorched limes, burst through the air. I knew the smell. It was demonic fury. At the same moment a ripple of darkness passed through the image of Harper's sister. Something black burst from inside her and exploded outward.

I lunged forward, throwing my body over Sariel's. He crumpled under me as I felt dozens of tiny blades slash through the back of my coat and shirt. The razor edges knocked me forward as they drove deep through my coat and skin. I stumbled down to my knees. I smelled my own flesh searing. A breathless shout of agony escaped me. Fires burst up along the edges of my torn coat.

Then suddenly a stinging wetness splashed across my back. The horrific burning stopped. I gasped for a breath and tasted something metallic. Liquid poured down my back, mixing with my blood. In a circle around me, glittering black slivers fizzed and melted into the pool of liquid.

"Are you all right?" Harper knelt down beside me.

"What did you do?" I asked, still too shocked to guess. From the stinging and the metallic smell, I should have known.

"Silver-water," Harper said. "I always carry a few vials with me, in case things get ugly. I'm sorry if it stung you, but I thought that would be better than what seemed to be happening."

"Yes, I think so," I said.

Beneath me, Sariel opened his eyes and swallowed slowly. He coughed and I moved aside so he could sit up. He pulled himself upright and then leaned back against the wall. For several minutes he simply stared up at the ceiling and took in slow steady breaths.

"I believe," Sariel said at last, "that we have come to the end of this line of questioning."

"What about Joan?" Harper asked.

"If you had any sense at all, you'd let her go." Sariel clenched his burned, bleeding hand to his chest. "Didn't you see what just happened?"

"But she is alive," Harper demanded.

"Yes, for what that's worth. You have no idea of the kind of fury that gives rise to an attack like that one," Sariel said.

"Do you know where she is?" Harper pressed.

"No." Sariel shook his head. "But if you plan on pursuing this any further, I'd ask that you leave me out of the matter. I think that more than enough Prodigals have died for you and your sister."

Harper frowned. Then he stood and straightened his coat.

"Thank you for your time, Mr. Sariel," he said. Harper walked to the door and then glanced back at me.

I could hardly think for the biting pain that lanced across my back. I started to stand but Sariel caught my hand. His touch caught my attention, for a moment overwhelming even my pain. His fingers were warm and gentle. I should have found comfort in that, but I couldn't.

"I forgave you years ago," he whispered.

"I know." I stood. "That makes it all the worse, really."

Sariel turned away from me. He wouldn't beg. I wouldn't have wanted him to.

I left with Harper.

Chapter Six
Ophorium

*T*he deep cuts in my back and the bubbling corrosion of the silver-water pooled into a single unyielding pain. I could not disentangle them. I could not separate the sharp stings of my sliced skin from the memories of older wounds. Each aspect of my pain touched another and bled into it until they formed a seamless fabric that enfolded me.

I didn't accept Harper's offer to clean me up. I turned him away at my door and stumbled up the stairs to my rooms in a daze. On the walk back from Hells Below, I had hardly seen or heard Harper. I recalled hazily that he had wiped away the foaming mass of blood that dribbled down my back. The rest of the world was lost to me.

My own hurt wound around me, weaving past into present. The jagged memories that I had carefully cut out of my thoughts suddenly poured their fury into my torn flesh. Inside my rooms I dropped to my knees and pressed my face hard into the cool wood of the floor. My muscles were shaking too much to let me stand, but I couldn't bear to press my back into any of my chairs or pillows. I knelt on the floor as time and memories bled into each other.

My suffering at the hands of the Inquisition had been far worse than this. But then, I had not known it could break me. I had believed in my own courage and my will. I had thought I was a strong man, incapable of betrayal. Then the prayer engines had begun their steady slicing into my flesh. Silver-water had been ignited in the bleeding furrows, searing each holy letter into my skin. Thousands of tiny white scars still traced the flesh of my arms, back, chest, and groin. They were marks of my cowardice, impressed into me like delicate watermarks.

I had thought that I was stronger than pain. Even stretched on the table, bleeding and burning, I had believed that I would never utter Sariel's name. But I had not known myself. I had not understood the Inquisition either, but they had certainly known me. They dealt in my kind. Thousands of us had come through their doors and been worked through like bank sums. I was no new mystery to the Inquisition; they simply slipped me into their mechanisms and opened me up like an oyster.

The prayer engines' needles had not always been packed with silver-water. Between days of burning agony they had given me sweet stinging pleasure. They had traced my body with rushes of ophorium and let me learn how deeply I loved its respite. In the end they hadn't needed to threaten me with pain; they had simply withheld my pleasure. I had given them Sariel's name.

Now I knelt on the floor and all I could think of were those long hypodermics sliding deep into my veins. Drops of blood wound down my ribs and spattered the floorboards. My back pulsed with the ache of Harper's silver-water and the remembered pain of those months under the prayer engines.

I hated it. I wanted away from every sensation of my body and every memory in my head. I wanted to escape, to somehow slip back into the furthest recesses of the past and forget every detail of myself. Slowly, I crawled to the desk where my needles lay waiting for me.

Chapter Seven
Fire

*T*wo hours later, the night blossomed. The sky unfolded in rich waves of purple and blue velvet. Breezes traced pale violet ribbons through the darkness. Tiny buds of glittering stars burst into brilliant illuminations.

I pushed my window open and leaned out. The moon spread its light across my face and bare chest. Wind rolled up through my hair and stroked my skin. When I had been a child, every night had seemed as lush and wondrous as this.

I glanced back into my room. The remains of my bloodstained shirt lay on the floor. My used hypodermic floated in an old cup of water along with a wilting dahlia. The choice between the night air and my filthy room was simple.

I shifted sideways and pulled my legs out so that I sat on the edge of my windowsill. I glanced down at the empty street below. Even the alley cats seemed to have gone to sleep.

Taking a deep breath, I threw myself out into the open air. Wind whipped over my bare skin and through my hair as I plunged downward. I smelled the filth of the ground below wafting up toward my face. A rush of terror and exhilaration shot through me.

With a twist of my body I veered up, turning suddenly from the mucky street and arching up into the vast sky. Giddy pleasure shot through my body. I swept up over a factory roof and caught hold of one of the tin chimneys. My momentum whipped me around it twice. When I let go, I went spinning off like a top.

I was well out over the butcher district before my momentum ebbed and I began to drift on the gentle night winds. For a while I rolled onto my back and stared up at the stars and moon. They seemed close enough for me to reach out and scratch my initials into their shining surfaces.

When I had been very young, I had snuck up from Hells Below to drift up into the open night. I had thought that it was my kingdom. For a few weeks I had thought that perhaps I was the secret child of an angel. I had floated up into the frigid mists of clouds and imagined that the moon, shining above me, was my promised halo.

When my mother noticed my frostbitten ears, she knew exactly where I had been. She sewed lead-shot into my nightshirt and told me that the heavens were not for my kind. We Prodigals were cast from hot molten fires, far below the realms of Man. The fact that a few of us could soar into the frigid heavens was simply a joke that God played upon us, tempting us to our deaths. But I had not been able resist the skies.

A low wind pulled me along past the window of a townhouse. I peered into a dim room. There were two little white beds, and I could make out the sleeping faces of the children tucked into them. I floated past the window and up to the roof. Beneath me, the family dog barked wildly. A man shouted at the animal and then slammed his window shut.

Once I was up on the roof, I took another dive, feeding the rush of my fear into a surge of flight. I zipped out across the White River and caught the updrafts over the water. I spread out my arms and hung above the city, just watching its dark mass. The factory district looked like an ugly rash that had spilled up from the insides of the earth. A sickly smell drifted off of it.

But above the White River, the stars cast glittering reflections over the rolling waters. Moored fishing boats silently swayed with the currents. I drifted, riding the wind up toward the Crown Tower Bridge. I felt a strange twinge as I drew closer to the massive structure. Across the west side of that bridge, Joan Talbott had been abducted.

I had no feeling for her. My only contact with her had come through the men around her. I had read Peter Roffcale's letters, listened to Edward Talbott's despair, and joined Harper in his search for her. I only felt her presence in the ruined wake of her disappearance. Roffcale had died. Edward Talbott had been willing to spend every coin he had to see her returned. Harper had hardly eaten or slept. I wondered how she could have inspired such love. What kind of creature was she?

I remembered her luminous eyes and long silken hair. Even conjured from wisps of smoke, she had been strikingly beautiful. I supposed that it would only be natural for men to adore such a woman.

I felt a burst of disdain and envy. I couldn't help but think that her life must have been pleasant and easy. Recalling Peter Roffcale's gutted corpse, I supposed Joan's life wasn't all that pleasant for her now, if she were still alive. It was petty of me, but the thought made me feel better.

Across the west side of the city, cathedral towers and ornate houses dominated the view. Suddenly I caught a flash from one of the city watchtowers. A searchlight ignited. A moment later, the piercing light swept across the cityscape. I dived quickly down, pressing my body against the supports of the Crown Tower Bridge. The last thing I needed was to end up netted by the Inquisition.

The spotlight swept past me and shot out over St. Christopher's Park. Two more lights split the night and turned to the park also. The lights swung through each other and across the air, searching. I kicked off the iron beams and glided down to the west end of the bridge. I ducked under the eaves of a house when a light slashed through the darkness near me. I knew I should drop back to the ground and just walk home.

Instead, I floated even closer in toward St. Christopher's. I couldn't help it. I wanted to know what other Prodigal had dared to take to the wind. Only a few Prodigals could fly. We were rare and growing more so with each generation. Sariel had been the only other Prodigal I had known who could soar into the dark sky. We had flown out of joy and instinct, believing that we were too high for any hand to reach. Neither of us had known how to evade the searchlights or nets. We had both ended up in St. Augustine's School for the Reform of Prodigal Youths.

One of the searchlights swept across the elegant houses on the south side of the park. For a moment, a black silhouette was captured in the light. The thin figure seemed frozen, pressed against a window. Then it dived. Four more searchlights cut through the air beneath the first. The Prodigal veered between them and fled into the wooded paths of the park. Another three lights came on. They closed in over the park. Below the searchlights, I could see lines of Inquisition men working through the bushes with their lime torches. The darkness was ripped into tatters as light after light sliced between the branches of trees and across the plots of flowers.

I dropped to the rooftops and ran across them, jumping from one to the next as I went. The closest watchtower stood only three roofs away. Once I passed it I would be in the circle of searchlights. I knew it was not my nature to run to the rescue of some idiot child. Still, I rushed in as if it were my own life I was saving.

The Inquisition men were already deep into the park. They were well ahead of me, but I had the advantage of the night itself. I could see into the shadows that they mistook for branches and twigs. I knew exactly where I needed to go. It was only a matter moving between the dozens of Inquisition men and their piercing lights.

A tense excitement pulsed through my body. I moved in behind one man, matching my steps to his. As he turned, I slipped up to the man just ahead of him. I was so close I could see the short hairs at the back of his neck. I could have slit his throat before he knew I was there. I held my breath. As the Inquisitor passed another of his own men, I switched off again. I moved with each of them, pairing and parting like a spreading disease.

At last I stopped. Slowly, I knelt down. The little Prodigal had been smart enough to know that the Inquisition men were expecting to find her up in the tree branches. Instead she crouched low, camouflaging her form in the lush shadows of irises and tulips.

She froze absolutely still as I knelt in front of her. She was small and filthy. Her short hair was caked with mud and her clothes smelled like rotting leaves. Tiny flickers of red fire moved through her dark eyes as she watched me. She looked like the kind of girl who bit men's fingers off. I held out my hand, letting her see my long black nails clearly. Then I raised a finger to my lips and stood back up. The rest I left to her. If she chose, she could remain hidden where she was. I was willing to offer her my help, but I wasn't going to force it on her.

As I began making my way back across the park, I glanced over my shoulder. She was following me. I didn't slow down for her or wait when she fell behind. I took care of myself. My attention circled between the movements of the men around me and the slashing searchlights overhead. I darted into shadows, then bolted from them moments before the sweeping lights burned them away.

All I offered the Prodigal girl was a chance to learn what I knew. I showed her the way out, but it was up to her to get through. She had to be quick and silent. One step in the wrong place and she would be trapped under dozens of hook-nets. Then the Inquisition would have her. She had no second chances.

When I reached St. Christopher's Cathedral, I bounded up into an alcove of sacred statues. A cluster of sleeping pigeons broke apart and flew up into the eaves. I leaned back against one of the weathered stone angels and watched the Inquisition's search. The lights continued to probe through the lines of trees and flash up into the cloudless night sky.

I didn't really expect the girl to follow me. When she floated up into the cranny next to me, I said nothing. I kept looking out across the park. I wondered if Harper lived in one of those houses.

"Do I know you?" the girl asked.

"I doubt it," I replied.

She was small, but older than I had first thought. Her expressions were hard and suspicious. I noticed the hilt of a knife jutting up from her belt. Her fingertips remained close to the knife as she watched me.

I turned my attention up into the dark sky. Above us, the stars still shone like jewels. Their luminescent colors shimmered and twisted with the distortions of the winds. The night was still deep and beautiful, but I couldn't seem to lose myself in it.

I watched a bat swoop through the air and snap up a firefly.

"Why did you help me?" the girl asked.

I didn't answer.

It was none of her business. She wasn't really the one I had wanted to save from the nets. My kindness had nothing to do with this girl, here now. It had just been a drug-addled attempt to comfort my own past. No one had come to my rescue when I had been trapped by the Inquisition. No one had been there for Sariel. So, years too late, I had come, as if I could somehow redeem either of us by saving this girl. I felt disgusted by my own sentimentality.

I scratched one of my black nails hard against the tip of a stone angel's wing. It left a white scrape, but nothing more.

"Are you a member of Good Commons?" the girl asked. The fissures of red fire in her eyes pulsed wider.

At the mention of Good Commons, I knew my escape into the sweetness of ophorium and the depths of the night had been futile. I couldn't out-distance the world that surrounded me. At every turn it seemed to close in over me. Still, I refused to abandon my night of thoughtless beauty. I pointedly gazed up at the North Star. Its blue brilliance burned into my eyes.

"Look at it." I pointed into the sky. "All it has to do is shine. Simply hang there in the sky and shine."

"Is this some kind of game?" the girl demanded.

"No."

"Are you drunk?" she asked suddenly.

"I wish I were," I said.

"You aren't with Good Commons?" she asked again.

I gave up. This girl just wasn't going to go away. I had made the great error of being kind to her, and because of that, she doubtless felt that there had to be some connection between us.

"I helped you because I thought it might have been a good thing to do for another Prodigal. I had no other reason beyond that," I said.

I frowned at one of the cathedral angels. Its face and shoulders were thick and distorted from the months of accumulated pigeon shit.

The girl studied me intently for a moment, then let her fingers fall back from the hilt of her knife. She looked out over the park. Inquisitors still searched the trees and undergrowth. She smiled, watching them.

"Do you know why I came here?" the girl asked.

"You came to do harm," I replied.

The girl's eyes narrowed. "What makes you think that?"

"You're carrying one knife in your belt and another in your boot." I took a small sniff of the air between us. There was a strong scent like that of scorched limes: sweet, bitter, and burning. "You're sweating vengeance. But what gives you away the most are your eyes. They've split. Red fires are shining through the cracks."

She looked surprised. She instinctively lifted her hand to her dirty face, then stopped. There was nothing she could do about it now. Slowly, she turned back to watch the movements in the park.

I looked back up into the sky. The ophorium ran thin through my bloodstream now. Flight and concentration had burned it to little more than vapor. I felt strangely cold, and everything around me seemed slightly ugly.

The shifting breeze caught the reek of rotting fish and sewage from the edge of the river. The moon seemed to have yellowed and cracked like a rotten tooth. Even the North Star took on the tawdry shine of costume jewelry.

"They murdered my friends," the girl said quietly. "One after another. Lily, Rose, Peter—"

"Peter Roffcale?" I asked softly. I knew it had to be him.

"Yes. Did you know him?" she asked.

"Just in passing," I replied.

"They strung him up and gutted him." The red fissures in the girl's eyes spread, swallowing her dark irises. Blood-red tears welled in her eyes and slid down her cheeks. "They gutted him like a fish. Like an animal. They did the same thing to the others, to Lily, to Rose..." She wiped her tears, smearing bloody slashes across the back of her hand. "I tried to stop them tonight, but I got there too late. They murdered Tom. He was just a boy." More bloody tears dribbled down her cheeks, and she scrubbed at them angrily.

"I'm sorry," I said. The girl hardly heard me.

"They'll pay. I'm going to make them pay. I don't care if I have to go to hell to do it. I'm going to kill them all." She stood up and glared down at the Inquisition men in the park. Slowly, her gaze moved on to the houses on the south side of the park. I remembered that I had first seen her floating just outside the window of one of those houses.

"Does one of them live there?" I studied the elegant building.

"No." Her expression softened momentarily. "The man who lives in that house has never done anything wrong to anyone. His only crime was to marry a coward."

Fury began to burn through the tones of her voice. "A weak, lying bitch who should never have been born. She should've been wiped off the face of the earth."

I felt the change in the air as the girl spoke. The smell of burning lime intensified to the sickening scent of acid. The familiarity of it made the wounds across my back shudder with remembered agony. The same sharp scent had come just before the attack against Sariel's conjuring.

"If you want to do a good deed tonight, you'll make sure that the Inquisitors get him out of that house."

The girl didn't spare me a glance. She whipped out her knife and spat on the blade. The steel blade turned instantly black and flames sprang up. She hurled the knife out into the sky. It streaked through the air and slashed through a window on the second story. An instant later, yellow flames exploded up, shattering the glass and tearing through the shingles of the roof. Black and violet clouds of smoke curled up into the air.

I glanced at the girl, but she had already kicked off the cathedral and swooped up into the night sky. The Inquisition men rushed to the fire. I watched. They pulled men and women out of the house, most of them servants. The timbers of the roof began to collapse, and a huge geyser of fire leapt up into the open air. I floated up on the hot currents.

Even through the thick smoke and waves of heat, I recognized the last man to be dragged from the burning house. For a moment,

I lingered on the searing currents. Below me the searchlights uselessly raked the thick walls of smoke. Down in the midst of the confusion and shouting, Edward Talbott stood in his nightshirt, watching the flames consume his home.

Chapter Eight
Smoke

I knew nothing about Joan Talbott except that her Prodigal friends were dying. Now her husband's house was in flames. Violent devastation seemed to encircle the woman, sweeping away those nearest her while she remained a mystery at the center of it all.

The smell of fire and smoke permeated my clothes. It hung in my hair, mouth, and nostrils and lay against my skin like a sheen of perfume. I wiped my face and kept walking. I wanted to think, clearly and calmly. Too much was happening, too quickly.

I needed to know more about Joan Talbott. Why had she inspired such hatred from a single Prodigal girl? Where had she gone, and how was she tied to Peter Roffcale's murder? I needed to find out what she had actually done in Good Commons.

All of these questions churned through my thoughts, but I couldn't concentrate on any one of them. They aroused flickers of my curiosity. But I was tired and too disconnected from them. They seemed like they should fit together, like they did, but I was missing just the right angle to slip them into place.

I toyed with possibilities, not because I thought I could solve anything, but to distract myself from another thought. I took in a long breath. The flavor of burning wood and the heat of full, rich flames rolled up through my thoughts. The smoking remains of Edward Talbott's house lay far behind me. The scent and sensation arose from my own memories of Sariel. Everything about fire reminded me of him. Now the scent of burning clung to me like a ghost, and I could not stop thinking of him.

I had kept memories of him buried for so long and so well that I had imagined that I had forgotten about him altogether. It had been a lie I wanted desperately to believe, and so I had.

But now, the very air seemed saturated with his presence. There was some detail in every object that I touched or passed that recalled a memory of Sariel.

The hiss and gurgle of the gas lamps reminded me of the way he had whispered curses constantly behind the backs of his least favorite teachers. He had also whispered, in that same quiet way, after he had fallen asleep in my arms. The low moaning of cats made me remember suddenly the first night we had made love. It had been in an alley, and neither of us had known very well what we were doing.

The smell of him seemed to rise through the wind. I closed my eyes and took in another deep breath. Above the reek of the horse shit in the street, there was that deeply familiar scent. I opened my eyes. It wasn't simply my haunted imagination; Sariel's presence twisted through the wind. He was nearby.

Unconsciously, I had been wandering toward him. I had followed his scent, all the while attempting to think about something else. I supposed it was in keeping with my deceptive nature that I should have lied even to myself.

The thin wisps of cigarette smoke drifted up against the dark sky. I followed them easily. Even among my own kind, my sense of smell was powerful. I found Sariel long before he caught sight of me. He strolled up Butcher Street as if it were his. A cigarette hung between his fingers. He exhaled, whispering softly as the smoke blew past his lips. His long green coat flapped slightly in the breeze, and the dark scarf he wore waved back behind him. The smoke rolled ahead of him, and he followed it.

He was beautiful. I had taken that for granted when I had known him before. His languid motions and bright eyes had been so familiar to me that I had not really known how rare he was. I had never understood why the headmaster at St. Augustine's insisted that Sariel keep his tempting glances to himself. He had simply been Sariel, and I had loved him. Now I realized how handsome he truly was. At the same time, I did not overlook Sariel's wickedly sharp black nails or his fixed expression of superiority.

He took a long drag off his cigarette. The fire in it burned bright red. After a moment of gazing up at the sky, Sariel released the white smoke in a long whisper. I felt him say my name; the pulse of his breath washed over me.

The exhaled smoke rushed up from Sariel's lips. It shifted and twisted as the wind moved through it, but it always wound its way back to the rooftop where I sat. Sariel watched it move, and at last he saw me. He came forward slowly, his outward calm betrayed only by the words he had burned into the air with such intense force.

The tongues of Sariel's smoke curled over me. They were warm and smooth, like delicate fingers. Wisps rolled over my bare stomach and shoulders. Sariel smiled at me and then soared up to the rooftop.

"Hello, Belimai," he said, and he flicked his dying cigarette back down to the muddy street. "Mind if I join you?"

"Do as you please," I replied.

Sariel sat down on the roof tiles and leaned back against the brick column of the chimney. We watched each other in silence for a few moments. He lit another cigarette.

"How's your back?" he asked.

"It's all right, so long as I don't think about it."

"You always were tougher than you looked." He frowned, then took another drag off his cigarette.

I watched the smoke he exhaled rise and twist up into the night sky.

"Were you looking for me?" I asked at last.

"Was it obvious?" he asked, and then he went on. "I wanted to say something to you."

"Oh?" I cocked my head slightly. "What?"

"Something. Anything. I just wanted to see you again, to say something more than goodbye," Sariel said.

I couldn't think of a response that didn't sound clever or cruel, so I kept quiet. Sariel smoked and at last crushed out the butt of his cigarette against the roof.

"You aren't going to make this easy, are you?" Sariel asked.

"What do you mean?" I watched the last thin streaks of Sariel's smoke turn on the night air.

"Don't do this, Belimai," Sariel said. "If you're angry at me, then say so. Scream at me if you want, but don't treat me like a stranger. Don't pretend that I'm some stray off the street who you've never seen before."

"I thought it would be better for both of us this way," I said at last.

"Better?" Sariel shook his head. "I'd rather have you beat my head in. At least then I'd know that you still felt something for me."

"I'm not going to beat your head in. I'm not even angry at you."

"How could you not be?" Sariel looked at me as if I were lying.

"I'm just not," I snapped. "What happened was my fault. How could I be angry with you?"

"It never occurred to you that I got you dragged into the Inquisition in the first place?" Sariel pulled a cigarette case out of his coat pocket, took one of the cigarettes, and lit it with a snap of his black nails. "If I had gone straight right after school, like you did, it never would have happened. We could have set up house, and maybe you would have gotten into that school…" He paused to exhale a long swirl of smoke. "What was it called?"

"I don't remember," I replied.

"Like hell you don't remember." Sariel stretched out onto his side and looked out at the sky. "It was the Downing Academy, wasn't it?"

"It's old history, Sariel. It doesn't matter what school. There's no point in trying to get me mad at you about something that's long past."

"You've avoided me for six fucking years, Belimai." Sariel jabbed his burning cigarette in my direction. "You're barely speaking to me now. It's not over. It's still going on right now between us. You think that I'm furious because you turned me in. And I think you hate me because…well, you're acting like it."

"I don't hate you, and I don't think you're furious at me." I shook my head.

"Then why did you stay away so long? Why did you leave Hells Below?" Sariel demanded.

"I changed." I knew that didn't make much sense, but there was no way that I could describe what had happened to me in the Inquisition. It hadn't just been the matter of a few scars and twenty pounds. I had been brought in as a proud youth, and I came out a pathetic addict. I might as well have been killed and my name given to a mongrel who resembled me around the eyes and jaw.

"You changed?" Sariel blew a hot tongue of smoke into my face and I glared at him. "Same nasty look, same vicious glare. You don't seem changed."

"I don't...Look at me, Sariel." I thrust my upturned arms out at him. "Open your eyes and actually look at me."

Sariel stared into my eyes for several moments. Slowly, his gaze moved over my dirty face. He glanced to my bare chest and at the white scars there. He followed the white letters over my shoulders and then down my arms. His expression was gentle until the moment he caught sight of the bruised, deep furrows that years of needles had left on both my arms. He looked away, but not before I saw an expression of revulsion flicker across his handsome face.

I folded my arms back in across my chest. I had invited his gaze to force him to admit that I was a wreck of what I had been. Still, the moment he glanced away from me, rejection knifed through me like a deep wound. It was what I had expected—demanded, even—but still it hurt me.

"You just need a bath and some rest," Sariel said, but he couldn't bring himself to look into my face.

"I know what I need, Sariel. In fact, I need it more than I need you." My bitterness at him made my words come out more harshly than I had wanted. "Don't patronize me with that 'all the boy needs is a bath, a bed, and a hot meal.' Save it for your Good Commons gatherings. I know perfectly well what kind of man I am."

"It isn't who you are; it's only what the Inquisition did to you." He was sitting up now, his red eyes glowing almost as brightly as the cherry of his cigarette.

"They took you in three times before they came after me, and you're the same as ever," I responded as coldly as I could manage.

"That's because I just confessed. I told them what they wanted to know, and I paid my fines." Sariel glared at me. "What were you thinking, trying to hold out?"

"I promised you I wouldn't betray you."

"It was only a fucking fine, Belimai!" Sariel was shouting now. "Fifty coins! Didn't you think I would have paid fifty coins just to not have you hurt? Did you think I was that cheap?"

"I didn't know what the charges were," I snapped. "I didn't know, and I didn't want you to end up roasting at the stake because I—" I cut myself short, realizing that this whole thing was going wrong. I closed my eyes and took a deep breath. All of this was over. It had come and gone. Screaming at Sariel now wouldn't alter even a moment of the past. Not even his one glance of repulsion could be taken back, now.

"I'm too tired to fight with you, Sariel. And I don't want to, in any case," I said.

"Neither do I." Sariel leaned back again. "Fighting is about the last thing I want, honestly."

He took a drag off his cigarette, and I looked up at the sky. The stars were still shining brightly, though a pale blue light crept up from the horizon.

"It's a nice night, isn't it?" Sariel asked at last.

"Yes," I agreed.

"Can we start over?" Sariel asked, and I knew he meant more than the conversation.

I wanted to tell him that we could. But the past could no more be forgotten than it could be undone. It would always be between us. When I looked at him, I could not help but remember who I had been and how low I had sunk since then. No matter how many years passed, I knew that I would never be able to think of him without recalling my time under the prayer engines. He would think of the same things when he saw me.

"No," I said. "Let's just go on."

A few more moments of silence passed. Sariel blew smoke rings, and then as a thick plume of smoke floated up from between his lips, he whispered the word, "Moth." The smoke curled into the form of a gypsy moth. Its wings beat against the breezes, dissipating as it rose up.

I smiled. Creating smoky moths had been the first magic Sariel had accomplished. He had shown them to me on a night much like this one, when the two of us had snuck up to the roof of the school. I remembered how his young face had been flushed with exertion and pride. He had singed his hair and burnt one of his fingers, but that had hardly mattered to him. Now he made it look as effortless as breathing.

Sariel leaned languidly on one elbow, as if he were on the edge of sleep. He watched me, but from the shadows of his lowered eyes. I didn't catch the word that he whispered, but the smoke that rose from his mouth whirled up into two slender forms. They circled each other, the thin trails of their bodies winding together. At last they drew into an embrace that swallowed them both.

Sariel looked directly at me then. As much as he wanted to return to the past, I needed to leave it behind. The man I was could never reclaim that time of trust and pride. I no longer fit into it. I looked past Sariel to where black walls of smoke still hung over Edward Talbott's house.

"Did you know Joan Talbott very well?" I asked.

"I knew her," Sariel said, "but we weren't associates outside of Good Commons. She was never willing to get her silk gloves that dirty."

"Tell me about her."

"What do you want to know?" Sariel looked slightly unsure of the turn of the conversation.

"What connection she had to Peter Roffcale and to a woman named Lily and another named Rose."

"So, Captain Harper really has hired you for his investigation." Sariel frowned. "I thought he might have just brought you along with him to protect himself."

"He hired me," I said. Whether to investigate, to provide a buffer from others of my own kind, or just to waste his money, I didn't know.

"Mica might have killed him if you hadn't been there." Sariel moved a little closer to me. "She raised Peter from the time he was nine. When we heard that he had been murdered, she...Well, you saw how she was. She's almost wasted away to nothing."

"Did Mica know Joan also?"

"Oh yes, they were fond of each other. I think Mica believed that eventually Joan would come back to Peter. She used to say that the girl was just scared. She needed time." Sariel shook his head. "Joan wrote a lot of our speeches, some of the best ones. But she never had the courage to deliver any of them or to attend any of the demonstrations. Peter and Lily read most of what she wrote. Rose took the vitriolic ones.

"Rose had a sweet look about her that let her say vicious things without losing the crowd. Peter did six months of labor for one of Joan's speeches. Lily spent ten months in a reformatory for Prodigal women. Rose was charged, but I think the judge couldn't bring himself to give her more than a fine. Even I've given speeches that Joan wrote. I was charged for public indecency for one." Sariel smiled briefly at this. "Joan, on the other hand, never even stepped into an Inquisition House unless it was to take a lunch to her half-brother—"

"Half-brother?" I asked.

"Captain William Harper," Sariel said, as if I should have already known that. "His father was some Inquisition abbot who got his head ripped off during the mine riots. Joan was the child from the mother's second marriage."

"I see."

"They're a rich family. Though you wouldn't know it from the captain. They own a huge estate house out past St. Bennet's. Before she married, Joan had a house up near the banks all to herself. She hired Peter on as an under-gardener. He carried her speeches down to us in Hells Below. I suppose he provided other services as well. It must have been quite nice for her. She could express her displeasure with the society around her while still enjoying its amenities."

"You sound like you hated her," I commented.

Sariel frowned a little, thinking about it.

"No," he decided, "I'm just bitter; perhaps, jealous. She had so much that the rest of us didn't. She was in a position to help many of us, but she was never willing to risk her own comfort. It's easy to get angry at her for that. But if I had been in her situation, I don't know that I would have done more. She did try to take part in a demonstration once."

"What happened?" I asked

"We broke into the Taylor Shirt workhouse and released twenty Prodigal children who were being rented out from a reformatory and forced to work. One of the shift foremen pulled the fire siren and the Inquisition rushed in on us. Joan was grabbed along with about ten others of us, but when we reached the Inquisition House, she was gone."

Sariel lifted his cigarette, then realized that it had burned down almost to his fingers. He flicked it to the street below.

So, the woman had disappeared more than once. I found that interesting.

"Do you think that Harper got her out?" I asked. It struck me as something he'd do.

"He could have." Sariel shrugged. "In any case, she didn't come back down to Hells Below. About three weeks later we found out that she had gotten married to Dr. Edward Talbott. They'd been engaged for a few months, but none of us had known. That was the last we heard from her."

"Peter Roffcale wrote to her," I said.

"I suppose he would have." Sariel looked down at his hands. "He never blamed her for leaving, but anyone could see that it tore him up to know she'd married another man."

"He mentioned that Rose and Lily had been murdered in one of his letters. Were there others?" I asked.

"Dozens. Members of Good Commons have been going missing or turning up in pieces for nearly a decade. One or two a year." Sariel flipped out another cigarette. He lit it and took a deep drag. "Recently, it's gotten worse. We used to make reports of missing persons. But since Peter was killed in custody, I think it's obvious that the Inquisition abbots don't give a damn."

Sariel's voice almost trembled with anger, then he stopped speaking. He simply stared up into the sky and drew in breath after breath of cigarette smoke. He had probably known all of the Prodigals who had been murdered. They would have been his friends and companions in Good Commons.

"I'm sorry," I said.

The words were embarrassingly worthless. My sympathy was as little good to Sariel as his forgiveness was to me.

"It happens," Sariel replied.

"Are you safe?" I couldn't help but ask. There was nothing I could offer him if he wasn't.

"No." Sariel smiled and shook his head. "None of us are ever safe, really. I've heard there's a sorcerer who sells potions made from Prodigal's bodies. He lures children away with candy and then chops them up and cooks them. There's also supposed to be a lord's club that requires every new member to kill a Prodigal as proof of his valor. Then there's always the Inquisition, over-zealous nuns, and simple, sick bastards. A lot of people seem to want Prodigals dead. The only protection we really have is each other." Sariel glanced over to me. "So, I'm safer than you, aren't I?"

"Maybe." I realized that I had made a mistake in asking after Sariel's safety. I shouldn't have left the impersonal inquiries about Joan Talbott.

"You never had any sense about how to look after yourself," Sariel went on. "You've gotten yourself into the company of an Inquisition captain. You're living alone, above ground—"

"Sariel, I've been living like this for six years. I've learned how to take care of myself."

"You can't always do it alone, Belimai. Sooner or later you're going to need someone else to help you." Sariel pulled himself a little closer to me. "Come back to Hells Below. There's room for you at Good Commons."

"You want me to join Good Commons?" I couldn't quite believe that Sariel was serious. Hadn't he understood what I had said to him, how deeply I had changed?

"You'd have friends there. You'd be involved in important work. We could help you come clean." Sariel placed his hand on mine.

A cold, almost nauseous sweat broke out across my skin. It wasn't just the thought of being with Sariel, constantly knowing that I had failed him. As a member of Good Commons, I would doubtless be brought into an Inquisition House again.

The well-oiled whir of the prayer engines hummed through my mind. The slashes across my back began to pulse with pain. The scars that covered my body ached. I pulled my hand from Sariel's.

"No, I think I'm a little too settled in my present life," I answered quickly.

I didn't care if he thought that my choice was a sign of the depths of my addiction. It was better than having him know the truth. Once, I had loved him enough to destroy myself for him. But I was no longer the same man. I was no longer that strong.

"It's nearly morning. I should go." I stood and walked to the edge of the roof.

"So, it's goodbye again?" Sariel asked.

"It has to be said sooner or later." I stepped off the roof and let myself drop lightly to the ground.

I heard Sariel's quiet goodbye from high above me, and I whispered my own in return. It was all that I had left to say to him.

Chapter Nine
Gloves

*M*orning light streamed into Harper's sitting room and reflected across his clean white walls. I flinched from the brightness, even behind the smoked lenses of my spectacles. Harper handed me a cup of coffee and sat down in a straight-backed chair across from me.

His hair was damp and clean. His clothes looked crisp. The freshness of his surroundings only exaggerated his exhaustion. Deep blue shadows stained the skin under his eyes. His lips were pale. Oddly, exhaustion seemed to suit him. I was growing used to seeing him looking worn out. It gave me a sense of knowing him to realize that I had expected to see him this way.

"How's your back this morning?" he asked.

"Not too bad." The cuts still hurt, but there was no point in dwelling on them. I drank a little of the coffee. It was bitter and too strong.

Harper poured cream into his coffee and then added three spoonfuls of sugar. He picked up the small, silver sugar spoon easily despite the black gloves that encased his hands. Sunlight glowed at his back, cutting a hard white line around his dark form.

"There was a fire at Edward's house last night," Harper said. "He was lucky that there were a dozen or more Inquisitors in the area when it broke out."

"It wasn't luck."

"What do you mean?" Harper asked

"I was there. I saw the girl who did it. She told me she wanted to make sure Edward got out of the house alive."

"What?" Harper stared at me in shock. It was pleasant to see such a strong reaction on his features. A moment later, and the expression was gone.

"Who was she?" Harper asked.

"She didn't tell me her name." I drank a little more of the hot, black coffee. "She was small. At first I thought she was a child, but when I got a good look at her, I realized she was full-grown. I think she might have been a member of Good Commons. She mentioned Lily and Rose, the same names that were in Peter Roffcale's letter to your sister."

"Lily Abaddon, Rose Hesper." Harper closed his eyes and rubbed his gloved hands across his forehead as if he were attempting to soothe a headache. "She probably was a member of Good Commons. What else did she say?"

"Not much. She wasn't in the best shape—"

"She was hurt?"

"Not physically, but she didn't seem too far from crazed." I poured several heaps of sugar into my coffee. "She said she tried to stop another murder but got there too late. A boy named Tom. Do you know anything about that?"

"Thomas Mills." Harper frowned. "We found his body last night, about an hour before the fire at Edward's house. The body had only been partially gutted. The girl must have interrupted the murderer before he could finish up."

"Murderers," I said. "She said they killed Tom. So that's more than one murderer."

"But she didn't mention any names?" Harper asked.

"No. She seemed to have other things on her mind."

I stirred my coffee while I thought about the Prodigal girl. Edward was blameless. If she did not want to harm Edward Talbott, then what had been the object of the fire? I wondered if she had known of Joan Talbott's disappearance.

"Was anyone harmed in the fire?" I asked Harper.

"Mercifully, no." Harper frowned just slightly. "In a way, I suppose that it's good that Joan is missing. The fire started in her empty room. If she had been there, I don't know how she would have survived."

"Do you think that could have been a coincidence?" It seemed unlikely to me.

"The fire starting in Joan's room?" Harper took another drink of his coffee. "I don't know. I've been too tired to think about it."

I didn't believe him. I hadn't noticed exhaustion keeping him from thinking about anything else. Still, if Harper wanted to keep his thoughts to himself, that was his right.

I had my own suspicion as to why the Prodigal girl had burned Edward Talbott's house. She wanted to punish Joan, to make the woman pay for abandoning the members of Good Commons. I wondered if the girl had believed, as Peter Roffcale seemed to, that Joan Talbott had some protection she could offer them.

"So, were you up all night?" I asked.

"Yes," Harper sighed. "After finding Thomas Mills and the fire, I couldn't sleep. I just spent the rest of the night going through old records."

"Perhaps you should try to get some sleep now." I set my cup of coffee down.

"No." Harper shook his head. "I managed to find one thing last night while I was looking through the records on Thomas Mills."

"He was in Good Commons?" I guessed.

"Yes, he was," Harper said. "But he also had a legal counselor by the name of Albert Scott-Beck."

The name meant nothing to me. I let Harper go on.

"Scott-Beck counseled Roffcale also. In fact, he visited him in his cell just an hour before you and I arrived."

"Do you think he murdered Roffcale?" I couldn't keep from leaning a little closer to Harper. The prospect of a solution drew me.

"Perhaps. I couldn't find any direct connection between Scott-Beck and Lily or Rose, however both women received legal counsel from his firm. Scott-Beck's partner, Lewis Brown, defended Lily when she was brought up on charges last spring. Brown also advised Rose a few months before that."

Harper drank a little more of his coffee.

"The firm takes on a good number of charity cases, mostly Prodigals who have no other means of legal defense at their trials. Almost every Prodigal in Good Commons has been defended or given counsel by Scott-Beck or Brown."

"Did either of them know your sister?" I asked.

"Joan?" Harper shook his head. His light hair was beginning to dry into loose curls. "She was never involved in any demonstrations or public readings. No charges could ever have been brought against her."

"So she had no connection to this Scott-Beck or his partner?"

"None," Harper replied. "To be honest, I don't even know that we're following the right trail to find Joan. But I can't just let these killings go on."

"It all seems too interlaced for your sister not to be somewhere in it," I commented.

"Perhaps."

There was something in the way Harper said the word that caught my attention. I wasn't sure if it was his tone or the word itself, but it reminded me of the night when we had first met and I had thought that Harper knew more than he was saying. I tried to study him, but the brilliant morning light burned at the fine details of his expression as well as the subtle scents that might have drifted off his lips. Some nights, if I concentrated, I could taste lies in the cool air.

This morning, all I had was a feeling of unease. I knew little about Harper, less about his abducted sister. The fact that she was abducted, while other members of Good Commons had been outrightly murdered, should have meant something. Yet I couldn't figure it out. There was something, a simple word, a small fact, that kept the matter from making sense.

I wondered if that word had been on Harper's lips when he held it back and offered me an oblique "perhaps."

I doubted that Harper was the only person who knew. I recalled the Prodigal girl's cracked eyes, her bleeding tears, and the smell of her. It was a horrific scent in comparison to the perfumes that had lingered on Joan Talbott's letters. Her hair had looked like it had been hacked off in a blind fury. Her clothes had been filthy ruins. I knew she hadn't burned Edward's house for nothing. She had known something about the murders and about Joan Talbott.

"So, will you go?" Harper asked, and I realized that I had not been listening to him.

"Where?" I asked, though it annoyed me to be caught so obviously adrift in my own thoughts.

"To Scott-Beck's office." Harper scowled at me. "You weren't listening at all, were you?"

"I was," I lied. "I just wanted to be sure."

"It wouldn't seem suspicious if a Prodigal like yourself were to ask some advice of his legal firm. It would be much simpler than convincing my abbot to give me a warrant for search. He doesn't believe that any of the Good Commons murders are worth our time." Harper frowned at his cup. "Some days I don't even know why I bother going in."

"The pay?" I offered.

Harper laughed at the suggestion.

"If I had joined the priesthood for money," Harper said, "I would have chosen one of the Golden orders, not the Inquisition."

I squinted at Harper through my dark spectacles, blurring his image. Most of the Bankers I had seen were soft pillows of men. They traveled in chubby little clusters like summer clouds drifting across the sky. I tried to imagine Harper dressed in the white robes of a Banker, his light hair forming a thin halo around shaved dome of his head. The image didn't hold beyond a moment's amusement.

I couldn't alter him, not even in my own mind. His lean body cut a hard, dark form against the light. He was a jarring blackness set against the white walls and polished elm of his home. Harper looked out of place even here in his own house.

It shouldn't have been important, but I knew Harper was keeping something from me. He seemed to be keeping something from the entire world. Even handling his own dishes, he wore gloves.

What was it that Harper wanted to hide so badly that he wouldn't even reveal himself in his own home? There were no personal photographs or paintings on the walls. There were no telling details, no books or childhood keepsakes, anywhere that I could see.

The only thing in the room that expressed Harper's presence was his own body. I stared into his brown eyes and wondered who he truly was. Harper stared back at me.

"I've lost you again, haven't I?" he asked.

"No," I replied. "I was just thinking that you haven't actually told me much about either yourself or your sister."

"There really isn't anything to tell." Harper stood up. "We ought to be on our way. I'd like to get you in to see Scott-Beck as soon as possible."

"That was a quick change of subject." I slowly pulled myself up from the chair.

"I'm too tired to be clever about it," Harper replied.

"Will you let me see your hands?" I asked.

"What?"

"Your hands." I pointed. "The things under the gloves. I'd like to see them."

"Why?"

"Because you want to hide them." I shrugged. "It's just the sort of person I am."

"You've already seen my hands." Harper lowered his voice, as if someone else might overhear us. "And a lot more of me."

"Then what's the harm in showing me again?" I asked.

"Why is it suddenly so important?" Harper asked.

"Your hands themselves aren't," I said. "Whether you show them to me or not, is."

"It's some kind of test?" Harper asked.

"Perhaps." I enjoyed using Harper's own word, though he didn't seem to note it.

Harper shook his head but went ahead and pulled off his gloves. He held his bare hands out in front of me. I studied them.

Very little about Harper seemed holy, but his hands were those of a saint. Pale and utterly flawless, they could have been cut from pearls. His long fingers stretched out in graceful curves. They were like virgin bodies, utterly untouched, even by the sun.

The urge to drag one of my black nails across the back of Harper's hand brushed through my thoughts. When I reached out and carefully touched one of Harper's fingers, I almost expected to see a dirty yellow stain left behind, but the skin remained flawless. I placed my palm against Harper's. His skin was warm and soft. I couldn't feel a single callus.

I glanced up to see his expression. He stared at me intently, waiting for my appraisal.

"Perfect." The word slipped out from me.

A smile flickered across Harper's lips. Gently, he slid his fingers down against my palm. He stroked the tender curve of my wrists and then curled his fingers up against mine. The lightness of his touch sent a shiver through my arms, and I caught another of his quick smiles.

"Your hands are perfect. Why would you want to wear gloves?" I asked, trying to draw my concentration away from the sensation of Harper's hands stroking mine.

"I don't know," Harper said. "My father always did."

"Did your stepfather wear them also?"

If I had wanted to catch Harper off guard, I couldn't have chosen a better way. For one brief moment he simply stood, frozen in place, looking as if I had sent an electric shock through him.

"I actually meant my stepfather," Harper said. "But how did you find out about him?"

"A friend mentioned him to me." I let Harper draw his hands back from mine without comment. When just our hands had touched, there had been an openness between us. We shared the honesty of simple physical pleasure. Sensation alone was easy to accept. It asked nothing. Once even a single question was raised between us, any illusion of trust fell away.

"Did your friend mention anything in particular about him?" Harper picked his gloves up from the tabletop.

"No. Should he have?"

"No," Harper replied firmly.

I had the distinct feeling that the conversation was at an end.

"It's time to go see Mr. Scott-Beck." Harper pulled the gloves over his hands and flexed his fingers against the black leather. His open palm closed again into the black fist of an Inquisitor.

Chapter Ten
Five Hours

O f course, I couldn't just see Mr. Scott-Beck. Not without a reference. I had to wait until he had an opening between his regular appointments. I slumped on a green loveseat in his waiting room. Other Prodigals passed me on the way in and then back out from their appointments. The wall clock chimed out a popular tune every half hour, and steadily I grew to hate it. I had nothing to do but wait and brood over the disassembly of that happy little clock.

I hoped that Harper was as bored as well, but I doubted it. He had decided to wait for me in the teahouse across from Scott-Beck's office building. When I looked out the window, I caught sight of him. He was talking to some blonde waiter. I frowned down at them for several minutes, then returned to my seat.

In the full face of boredom, I longed to drag up some scent of terror or bloodshed. For the first two hours my anticipation of danger kept me nervous and wary. I watched every movement of the secretary, every exchanged greeting and goodbye, as if it were a prelude to murder. But steadily, as I witnessed the flow of Prodigal after Prodigal through the firm's doors, my excitement waned into reason.

The fact that all of the murdered members of Good Commons had gone to this particular firm seemed damning until I realized that almost every living Prodigal seemed to use this firm. I wasn't even sure that any other legal office offered services for Prodigals. People came for dozens of different reasons. Some had wills, others needed contracts notarized, while still others were clearly criminal. I imagined that most of the population of Hells Below had come and gone through the firm's doors.

The clock on the wall rang out its sweet, happy melody, announcing yet another hour of my life wasted in this room. The waiting room exuded benign tedium. The chairs and loveseats were spread out in a loose circle along the walls, allowing clients just enough distance from each other to keep them quiet. A set of pallid watercolors hung on either side of the window, and on the wall behind me there was the incessant tick of the wall clock. The place exuded the palpable sensation of devouring hours that I would have rather spent doing almost anything else.

I gazed out the window. The blonde waiter was at Harper's table again. I couldn't see the waiter's face, but Harper gave him a slow, deep smile that made me think he must have been attractive. Fleetingly, I wished I had a rock to hurl at him.

I turned to the only other person in the waiting room with me at the moment. The office secretary looked back at me with all the charm of a halibut. I tried to study him with interest, imagining that somewhere behind his murky green eyes there might be the flicker of dark murderous longing. The secretary blinked and then returned to sorting the stacks of paper on his desk. His only deep desire seemed to be for proper filing.

No matter who came through the door, the secretary seemed to have a form for him to fill out. I had completed mine in the first minute of entering the room by simply leaving the questions unanswered and printing my name at the top of the page in the kind of deformed, clumsy script that screamed of illiteracy.

At the time, I had thought I was clever for so deftly eluding the paperwork, but now I regretted it. At least filling the form out would have used up a little of the empty time I now had. I might have been able to amuse myself by writing in deliberately obtuse answers and a few outright lies. Instead I jabbed quietly at the cushion of the loveseat with my hard, black fingernail, slowly gouging my initials into it.

When the clock chimed out its bright little tune for the tenth time, I realized with annoyance that I had the song memorized. At his desk, still sorting papers, the secretary hummed the tune aloud without seeming aware of it. I clawed at the loveseat with a little more force.

A man and wife came in together, both dressed in their church best. They eyed my attack on the loveseat and then seated themselves as far from me as possible. They peered at me but looked away before I might make eye contact. The secretary brought them a sheaf of papers to fill out. The couple complained about the trouble all this was and how it didn't seem right that they, who were the wronged party, ought to have to do so much. The secretary apologized without much feeling and then drifted back to his desk.

Every few minutes the husband or the wife stole a glance in my direction. They obviously believed themselves innocent in whatever legal matter had brought them to this office. I, on the other hand, clearly had the look of a hardened criminal of some kind. I heard the soft whispers of their speculations.

I leered at them and they pressed closer to each other, ignoring me with all their concentration.

"Sykes?" A middle-aged man called out from the door just past the secretary's desk. "Belahhh...Is there a Mr. Sykes here?" he asked, unable to make out the brutish scribble that I had given as my first name.

"Here." I stood and went to the man.

He was shorter than me by a few inches, but heavier. His shoulders and chest bowed outward in a thick mix of muscle and fat that reminded me of a bulldog. His animal physique looked odd packed into such an elegant suit. The image he cut was almost amusing, except that I got the distinct idea that the man could snap me in half if I laughed at him. Powerful men could dress however they liked.

A smell on him burned at my nostrils. It bothered me, but I couldn't pick it out from beneath the thick waves of cologne that hung around him like mosquito netting. As he shook my hand with a firm military grip, I noticed that two of his fingers were bandaged.

"Cats," he explained, though I hadn't asked. "I'm Lewis Brown,

Mr. Scott-Beck's partner. I've gotten through all of my appointments today, so Albert asked me if I could run you through the first interview." His voice was slightly too loud and, like his handshake, too assured to be natural.

"Thank you," I said when I realized that he was waiting for as much. I smiled to make up for my belated response. The only thing that truly pleased me was the prospect of escaping the waiting room before that clock went off again.

"Come along." Brown turned hard on his heel and strode back through the doorway. I followed him through, then up a steep flight of stairs. He moved quickly, as if reaching the top of the staircase was a venture to be relished with healthy enthusiasm. I lagged behind.

"I had a late night," I said after Brown turned and noticed that I was still several feet below him. "I'm still a little tired."

"You work nights, do you?" Brown placed both his thick hands on his hips and looked down at me from the top of the stairs.

"No, I was up with a girl." It pleased me to mislead Brown while telling him the truth. I reached the top of the stairs and followed Brown into his office. The room was large but filled with shelves of record books. Brown's desk was near the one window in the room. Late afternoon sun poured in between the curtains. I sat down across from Brown and shifted the chair so that I wasn't staring straight into the light.

"Well, let's begin with these questions first." Brown set the unanswered form with my scribbled name at the top down on his desk.

"Very well." I smiled to cover my lack of enthusiasm. The burning scent that had clung on Brown's gray suit seemed now to be drifting out from some corner of the room.

"Your full name," Brown said.

"Belimai Sykes," I replied, still half-lost attempting to recognize the smell.

"No middle name?" Brown asked.

"What? Oh, yes. Rimmon." The scent was distinctly coming from above the bookshelves. At first it almost smelled like rosewater, but the longer I remained in the room, the more I began to pick up sharp, searing undercurrents.

"Rimmon." Brown paused after he had written my name in on the form. "I assume that's your lineage name."

"I suppose." I forced myself to turn my attention back to Brown.

"Now let me see…" Brown thumped the back of his pen lightly against his chin. For a moment he looked as if he was reading from some text at the center of his empty desk. "Clothed in the darkness he came beside Sariel, his body white as the lightning, his voice a terrible thunder, and he was called Rimmon, and he too knelt before the cross…"

I just looked at Brown.

"Book of Prodigals," he said. "It's a hobby of mine, keeping genealogies of all those fallen princes. It's very telling, you know."

"Is it?" I wasn't really sure of what else to say. If I had had a genuine legal problem, I might have been annoyed by this digression. As it was, I thought it might be better than filling out the form. I let Brown go on.

"Yes, indeed. You may think that genealogy has little importance in this modern age, but many Prodigals still carry traits of their ancestors in one form or another." Brown looked me over for a moment. "You, for example, I would guess are one of those rarities, a flyer. You have a strong affinity for the air, either moving through it or smelling and tasting it." Brown made several marks on the form. "I'd also guess that you're pretty solitary, even among your own."

"All that from just a name?" I asked, neither acknowledging nor refuting the description.

"From just the name," Brown assured me with a look of pride. "Of course, there are well over a hundred names and attributes to keep straight in your head. I know most of the higher demons, but it's Albert who has all of them memorized perfectly."

"Mr. Scott-Beck?"

"Yes. The man has the memory of a mastodon." Brown turned back to the form. "Family?" he asked just as I had again begun to draw in curious tastes of the air in the office.

"No," I replied.

"None?" Brown seemed unable to credit this. "Certainly you have parents?"

"Both dead."

"Oh. Was it the Inquisition?" Brown asked with an unnatural gentleness in his voice. I could imagine him practicing that tone at night while flipping through the evening paper.

"No," I replied, though it was half a lie. "My father was killed after a mine collapse." The explanation had been my mother's way of lifting the criminal nature out of my father's execution for sabotaging the Wellton mining company. "My mother drowned during the sewer floods twelve years ago."

"And you have no one else?" Brown pressed.

"May I ask why you need to know?" I didn't mean to sound irritated, but the elusive smell in the room and the memory of my mother's bloated dead body had twisted into a single presence. Repulsion and sorrow for a moment made me wish to just get up and leave the room. I held my breath against the smell in the air and the feeling passed.

"We need someone to contact in case you're summoned to court and we can't find you," Brown explained.

"I see." I frowned. "I can't think of anyone. You'd just have to leave a word at my residence."

"And where is that?" Brown skipped down several spaces on the form.

"For now, the Good Commons Boarding House, in Hells Below." I watched Brown carefully as I gave my answer.

"Good Commons." He smiled just slightly at the corners of his mouth as he wrote the name. "Yes, I believe I know where that is." He didn't pause long enough to take a breath before asking, "So, do you already have a criminal record?"

"Yes."

"Then let's have a look, shall we?" He stood up and went to his shelves. I watched as he slowly paced past the first two shelves and then whipped one of the thick, black record books out.

"It would be under Sykes, would it?" Brown asked.

"Yes." Though I could see what he was obviously doing, I couldn't quite believe it. I glanced again at the shelves and shelves of record books that filled the room.

"Here it is." Brown sat back down behind his desk with the big book open. "Hmm, flying and resisting questioning." Brown looked curiously at the page and read on a little. "All that trouble just to keep your friend from getting a trespass fine." Brown looked up at me. "It took them quite a while to get his name out of you, didn't it?"

"You have a copy of my legal record?"

"Yes. Albert and the Brighton abbot are old school friends, so the abbot has been kind enough to let our firm keep copies of the records involving Prodigals." Brown flipped the page and then turned it back. "You don't have much of a record. It looks like you've managed to keep a step ahead of the law for the most part."

"For the most part, yes," I replied.

I knew in the back of my mind that there had to be records of my birth and education, even my arrests and time under the prayer engines, but I had imagined that all those things had been filed far away in some dark basement. I hated the idea that my life could be fingered through by a stranger at his leisure.

"You are quite the specimen, aren't you, Mr. Sykes?" Brown turned the book so I could see it. He taped his thick finger on a small tracing of a photograph. It took me a moment to recognize my own body stretched out on the table. I stared down at my own furious gaze without interest. My memories of that time were sharper than any smudgy drawing could ever be.

As quickly as I could, I read through the dozens of comments and tracings of my effects at the time of my arrest. I wanted to know what Brown or anyone else with access could know about me. The page was clotted with trivialities: my shoe size, fingernail lengths, a tracing of my business card, and a long string of initials where one officer or another had checked the record out. W. J. H. appeared a dozen or more times.

It only took a moment for me to realize where Harper had come across my business card. He would have known all of this about me before he even walked through my door. It shouldn't have surprised me.

Brown turned the book back to himself and read over it for a few more moments.

"His uncooperative nature and refusal to testify have put us in a position to assume guilt...Still no statement...Questioning with silver-water...Ah, and ophorium." Brown made a little clicking sound with his tongue. "Just to keep your friend from getting a fifty-coin fine? I'm not sure I would believe that myself. Were you holding out on something else?"

I stared at Brown flatly.

"I suppose if you wouldn't talk, then you won't just tell me now." Brown seemed amused. "You know, Mr. Sykes, if our firm is to represent you, it's in your best interest to tell us the full extent of anything you've done."

"I'll keep that in mind." I managed to get the words out civilly. The deep desire to slash Brown's face had seized me the moment he began reading from my record. Those months had been my ruin and he read over them as if they were prices on a menu. I closed my eyes and took a deep breath, trying to calm myself.

The scent and taste of acidic sickness, something between excrement and bile doused in heavy rose perfume, washed into my lungs. I coughed and Brown pushed the record book to the side of his desk.

"It's getting late," he said.

"Should I be going?" I started to stand but Brown held up his hand for me to stop.

"No, I'm sure Albert will want to speak with you." He smiled at me as if we were friends. "No, I was thinking that I ought to get a little something in me. I'll send Tim out for some supper. A little snack for you too." Brown stood and started for the door. "It'll be my treat. You just wait here. I won't be long." He stepped out and closed the door.

I waited a moment, then checked the door. Brown had locked me in.

Chapter Eleven
Blue Glass

*J*ust the fact that I had been locked in made me immediately want to escape. I walked to the window. It was painted shut, but the glass was thin enough to break through.

I stopped myself. Crashing through the second story window would be an act of desperate panic, a last resort. I wasn't sure that the situation merited that.

There were reasons other than murder that Lewis Brown would want to keep a Prodigal from roaming freely through the building. Brown could have just wanted to keep me from bumbling in on another interview. It was equally likely that he kept the door locked out of habit.

My instincts urged escape. I could easily knock out the glass with Brown's chair and be out. But my instincts weren't paying me to be here in the first place.

I looked down at the street and wished I could see Harper. The second story only provided me with a view of roofs and the tops of a dozen or more hats. Below me people made their ways back home. Offices and shops were closing. It would be night soon. The darkness drifting in over the sky calmed me.

I decided to investigate Brown's office and the disturbing smell that hung in it. I took a deep breath and spread my arms out. As I blew the air out of my lungs, I slowly drifted up. I continued to rise until my head lightly bumped into the ceiling.

The air near the ceiling was rank. I nearly gagged, and when I opened my eyes, they stung. The tops of Brown's shelves were filled with rows of blue glass jars. Some were large apothecary jars; others were smaller, perfume bottles. All of them were filled dark thick liquids.

I drifted closer to the jars. The smell was nauseating. I squeezed my nostrils closed with one hand and read the pieces of paper that were attached to the rows of blue bottles. One big container read, *Strength Beyond Numbers: Abaddon*. Another was marked, *Power to Churn the Waters: Rahab*. I frowned and scanned across the multitude of labels: *Beauty, Wealth, Control of Fire*, and even the *Lordship Over Insects* was cited, and a name written beneath that. Many of the bottles were nearly empty. But the one nearest me was completely full.

I picked up the small bottle, hardly larger than an ink vial. It was sealed with a waxed lid. Its paper label was crisp and white, still untouched by time. It said, *Prophecy: Roffcale*.

Holding the vial in my palm, I sank back down to the floor. I broke the wax seal and almost choked on the smell that seeped up. It was the same pungent scent that had pervaded the cell where Peter Roffcale had been murdered. Rosewater poured through the soured smell of his blood, urine, and shit.

Magic potions made from the bodies of Prodigals. Wasn't that what Sariel had said?

The door opened behind me, and I shoved the vial into my jacket pocket. I quickly turned to face the man who had entered the room. He was much taller than Brown, but just as muscular. His hair and beard were white, but he seemed youthfully fit in spite of that. His skin was tanned and flushed with a healthy glow. He smiled at me as if I were his favorite nephew.

"I'm truly sorry about the delay in meeting you, Mr. Sykes." The big man held out his hand. "I'm Albert Scott-Beck."

Out of habit I took his hand. He smiled even more brightly and didn't release my fingers from his tight warm grip.

"May I ask you a question, Mr. Sykes?" He was close enough that I could smell the blood and rose perfume on his breath. His fingers felt like steel shackles encasing my hand.

I remembered that the blue glass jar marked *Strength Beyond Numbers* had been nearly empty. I wondered how much of it Scott-Beck had running through his veins.

"Who sent you in here?" he asked.

His hand crushed brutally around mine. I slashed my free hand up and drove my long nails into the flesh of his throat. His skin was like horse hide. My claws barely cut into it.

In an instant, Scott-Beck stepped aside and twisted my hand violently. Cracking pain burst through my arm as a bone in my wrist snapped. He twisted my hand farther and I stumbled on my feet, dropping to one knee.

He kicked me hard in the chest. My ribs cracked inward. My lungs crushed in as the air was forced out of them.

"Who sent you, Mr. Sykes?" He was still smiling as if this had just been a friendly tussle.

"You're going to kill me whether I say or not, aren't you?" My voice was barely audible.

"Of course." Scott-Beck squeezed his fingers around my broken wrist. "But it's up to you, how I do it."

"Please, don't." I closed my eyes as if that would hold out the pain. "The man who hired me..." I carefully dropped the fingers of my free hand down into my coat pocket. "He didn't tell me his name, but he wore an anatomist's pin. He was blonde and young." I closed my hand around the vial.

"An anatomist?" For a moment Scott-Beck's attention shifted from me to the man who hired me.

I lunged forward, smashing the vial into Scott-Beck's groin. The delicate glass shattered and Scott-Beck howled in agony. I jerked my hand free of him and scrambled for the window.

A brutal weight slammed into my back and crushed me face down to the hard wood floor. I hadn't seen Brown come in after Scott-Beck, but I recognized the smell of him on top of me. I tried to twist out from under him, but his weight on top of me was immovable. He seized a fistful of my hair, jerking my head up. The tendons of my neck strained as he pulled my head back so that I was looking up at him.

"It seems that you still don't know how to answer a question properly, Mr. Sykes." Brown's face was flushed deep red. His expression was one of pleasure, almost arousal. He slammed the side of my face down into the floor. A deep explosion of pain and dizziness rocked through my skull. He pulled my head back up and slammed it down again. I fought against him. Brown threw his weight against my straining neck and my head cracked into the floor again.

My throat and shoulders spasmed with tearing pain. Blood welled out from the side of my head where my skin had split upon impact with the floor. My vision wavered as a ripple of darkness passed through my consciousness.

Brown lifted my face again, and this time I hung limply in his grip.

"What about it, Albert?" Brown asked. "Shall I split his little skull?"

"We want to know about the girl first." I heard Scott-Beck walk up on my left. "Ask him who she is."

"Well, then?" Brown shifted his weight on my back, rocking his groin against me as if I were a two-penny whore. "Where's the girl you've been working with, Sykes? What's her name?"

"I think it might be something like...Fuck You!" I could hardly think for the pain, but it didn't make me any more co-operative.

"Listen, Sykes. I can make you wish you were back in the Inquisition House." Brown pulled my head back a little more. I could see Scott-Beck out of the corner of my eye. He stroked his thick white beard and studied me. In my beaten state, I suddenly thought that he looked a great deal like a painting I had seen of Father Christmas. He considered me as if it pained him to see that I would be going down on his naughty list.

"I don't know how far you're going to get with him—" Scott-Beck's words were cut short by a sharp rap at the door.

Scott-Beck walked back out of my view, but Brown remained on top of me. I heard Scott-Beck open the door.

"What is it, Tim?"

"There's a man from the Inquisition here." The secretary sounded slightly flustered.

"What does he want?"

"He says he's looking for a Prodigal named Belimai Sykes." The secretary's voice dropped to a whisper. "He won't go away."

"How inconvenient." Scott-Beck walked back to where Brown had me pinned. He dropped down beside me and took a firm grasp on my throat with both his hands.

"Lewis," he said to Brown, "you and Tim go down and get rid of the Inquisitor. I'm afraid that we're not going to have all the time we would have liked with Mr. Sykes."

As Brown rose off of me, Scott-Beck lifted me by my throat. I scrambled to gain my footing. Brown caught my arms and jerked them back behind me. Pain seared through my broken wrist.

"I was hoping to have a little longer with him," Brown said.

"Next time," Scott-Beck assured him. "Perhaps with the girl."

"Fair enough." Brown retreated back through the door with the secretary.

Scott-Beck sighed and then shoved me back against the desk. His expression was resigned, not even slightly perturbed. I knew from the sheer number of bottles on the shelf above us that he had murdered many Prodigals before me. If it had ever troubled his conscience, he was long past that now. Like the Confessors who had tortured me in the Inquisition, he was utterly at ease with himself and what he did.

I hated Scott-Beck for that.

Rage gave me a burst of strength. I kicked him as hard as I could and shoved against him. Scott-Beck stumbled but caught himself before I could twist free. He slammed his fist into my bleeding head with professional ease.

My vision went entirely black. Blind nausea swelled through me, enveloping all other sensations of my body. I rolled back into a senseless darkness and collapsed onto the desk.

Often in the last six years I had thought of my own death as a comfort. I had thought of it as I slid a needle into my soft flesh and imagined that it would be as easy and restful as the ophorium that poured into my blood. But now I knew I didn't want to die. Too much had been taken from me already. My life was all I had to claim.

A burst of stabbing agony brought me back up. Scott-Beck was leaning over me with one hand planted directly on my throat. My shirt and vest had been torn aside, and a bowl was tucked up next to my bare chest. With his free hand, Scott-Beck continued to slice a scalpel deep into my stomach.

Fury surged through my body. I had never felt anything like this before. A deafening roar ripped up from my throat. The sound of it was like a thunder clap. The window exploded. Scott-Beck took a stunned step back, the scalpel falling from his fingers to the floor. For a moment I thought my scream alone had caused all the blood to drain from his face.

Then I felt the heat of flames bursting up across the floor. I turned my beaten face and saw the Prodigal girl from Saint Christopher's Park hovering just outside the open window. Scott-Beck took another quick step backwards.

The girl moved forward, crouching on the windowsill. Her cracked red eyes followed Scott-Beck's every motion. I didn't think she was even aware of my presence.

"I can smell his blood on you," she said to Scott-Beck. "You murdered Peter."

Scott-Beck started for the door. The girl was faster than him. She sprang into the air and hurled one of her black-bladed knives. Scott-Beck dropped to the floor. The knife whipped over his head and drove into the wall. Flames burst up from the blade and spread across the wallpaper.

Scott-Beck barely paused. He lunged to one of the far shelves and snatched a box off of it. The girl rushed after him.

I rolled off the desk but didn't have enough strength to support myself. I slid down onto the floor. Flames climbed up the desk and consumed the wall behind me. I glanced back at the window, but there was no way I could get through the fire to reach it. I grabbed the back of a chair and pulled myself up. The motion sent bursts of pain through my body, but I forced myself past it. Already the heat of the growing fire distorted the air. Smoke caught in my lungs. If I didn't get out, I was going to be burned alive.

I stood in time to see Scott-Beck grab the girl's leg as she sprang at him. He slammed her into the floor with a brutal, practiced force. Then I saw what he had gotten from the shelf. He had a pistol.

If he killed her, there was no chance I would get out of the burning office. I grabbed the scalpel Scott-Beck had dropped. Its metal body was searing hot, but the burn hardly registered against the waves of pain that ran through the rest of my body.

I hurled the scalpel so hard that I almost fell again. The blade sank deep into Scott-Beck's neck. He stared back at me in utter shock.

All it took was that moment. The Prodigal girl drove one of her knives into Scott-Beck's arm. The pistol fell from his hand and a shot rang out.

Then there was a second and a third. I realized that they had come from the stairs. The door burst open and Harper rushed into the room.

"Belimai!" he called, then he stopped dead still at the sight of the girl. "Joan?"

The girl didn't even look at him. She leapt back out of Scott-Beck's grasp and then hurled another blade into his chest.

"Joan! No!" Harper caught her and pulled her back from Scott-Beck. Even with Harper's holding her, the girl didn't spare him a glance. She kept her eyes on Scott-Beck alone.

The hilt of her knife jutted up from Scott-Beck's ribcage. It glowed as if it were molten. Scott-Beck grasped it, desperate to pull it free of his body. Flames burst up over his hand. For a moment the smoke in the room smelled strongly of roasting meat, and then geysers of white-hot flame exploded up through Scott-Beck's chest. The man's mouth opened as if to scream, but only flames came rushing up into the empty air.

The Prodigal girl smiled as if she were at a carnival.

"You'd better get your friend out of here, Will." She pulled away from Harper. "He's been hurt rather badly."

I thought Harper was going to say something more to her, but then he rushed forward to me.

"Can you walk?" he asked.

"A little." I swayed on my feet. The heat of the fire all around us was astounding. The smoke was beginning to bother my eyes. It was good that Harper had only been in the room for seconds. His body wasn't made to withstand this kind of heat and smoke. He coughed and wrapped his arm around me.

"Lean on me," he said.

I did. We got out of the room as fast as we could. The Prodigal girl just watched us and then floated up to the top of the shelves. I heard the sound of bottle after bottle smashing. Harper all but dragged me down the stairs. Halfway down he had to kick Brown's body out of his way. The secretary, Tim, lay with a bullet hole through his head at the foot of the stairs.

"Good shot," I muttered, but Harper didn't seem to hear me over the rising wail of the city fire sirens.

When we reached the street, dozens of Inquisitors were already gathered as well as Sisters from the Order of the Flame. Water pumps clanged and roared while the fire sirens continued to scream. Above us, explosive bursts of fire gushed through the windows and roof of the building. The smoke that poured out reeked of burning meat and rose perfume.

Harper laid me in the arms of one of the Sisters and turned back toward the burning building. I caught his arm, gripping it with the same hard force with which I clung to consciousness.

"You can let go now, Belimai," Harper said softly. "You're safe."

I dug my claws into Harper's coat sleeve, pulling him closer.

"She's gone," I whispered to him.

"You don't understand. I need evidence—" Harper was cut off as one of the Sisters pulled him back from me. I let go before my nails cut his skin.

Another of the Sisters moved in beside me. She hardly glanced at my face. To her I was only an assortment of wounds. Her eyes narrowed at the sight of my slashed stomach.

"He's losing blood." She pressed her hand over the wound. "Get me morphine and needles." Two young girls in white brought what she asked for immediately.

I realized, as the Sister to the left of me began to fill a syringe with morphine, that Harper had gone.

"Harper..." My voice barely carried above the chaos around me.

Inquisitors shouted at people to stay clear. Others barked orders to subordinates. The wheels of the water hoses and pumps chugged like train engines, and above it all the sirens continued to wail.

In their white caps and robes, the Sisters of the Order of the Flame closed around me like a wall. One of them lit a small lime torch. I flinched from the sudden brightness. A novice gently cradled my head back so that I was staring up into the sky.

I felt the familiar sting of a needle piercing my arm. The circle of Sisters closed in over my stomach. I distantly felt their fingers moving across my skin. I could hear one of them giving rapid orders, but the words themselves eluded me.

The pain and chill of my body began to slip away. I stared up into the night. High in the sky I thought I made out a thin black silhouette. A star shimmered behind her, and for a moment she seemed to flicker against the darkness like a single firefly.

I wondered if Harper saw her, or if she was looking down at him. Either way, the sight was not meant for me. I closed my eyes and let it go.

Chapter Twelve
Stitches and Alcohol

*T*he Sisters' threads were so thin and their stitches so tiny that it was hard to imagine how they alone had barred death from my body. The scars that remained after the stitches were removed were white and faint. The one that ran up my stomach was hardly visible. Only a dull ache lingered from my broken wrist. It seemed that my body longed to erase any traces of Scott-Beck's crimes.

The editors of the newspapers had done much the same. Their stories read like a tragedies. A man of deep compassion, Albert Scott-Beck, as well as his associate, Lewis Brown, and his secretary, Timothy Howard, had perished in a terrible fire. Scott-Beck left behind a grieving wife, two children, and many friends from all walks of life. Hundreds of Prodigals held a vigil in his memory, and many attended the services in his honor.

The world, the papers said, was a darker place for his loss.

I clipped out an article, scrawled the word *LIES* across it, and then added it to my most recent scrapbook. I should have been immune to the sinking feeling of futility by now, and yet I wasn't. I was half-sick thinking of Prodigals weeping for a man who had murdered their children and friends. Scott-Beck was on his way to being remembered as a hero to our kind.

I wondered what Harper thought of all this, then regretted it. I hadn't seen nor heard from Harper in nearly three weeks. He had gotten what he needed of me, though I doubted it had been to his satisfaction, and now he was gone. That was to be expected. I shook my head, disgusted with my own loneliness. I had never expected things to work out with Harper. There could be nothing between us once my job was done. That was simply the way the world was. Somehow, it still cut into me deeply.

The night outside was hot and thick with insects. My rooms seemed to resound with emptiness, despite the stacks of book and papers. They were only evidence of my solitude. In any case, I was out of ophorium and had been for a day. I had to go out sooner or later.

I trudged out and wandered the streets. The darkness hung around me, but it was not enough to allow me to forget myself. I wandered farther until I found a familiar staircase. I remembered the dog's head painted on the wall and descended down into the ale house. I knew I was hoping to see Harper there, but I didn't want to admit that, not even to myself.

When I didn't find him, I couldn't just turn around and leave. It would have brought my half-recognized motivation up into brazen acknowledgment. I bought a bottle of blue gin and sat down at one of the tables far in the back of the room. The gin tasted like paint thinner. I took a long drink straight from the bottle, just to catch myself up with the other men who swayed in their seats throughout the room.

Once the gin started to erode my senses, I began pouring myself shots and tossing them back at a more refined rate. I remembered that my mother had drunk this way right after my father had been executed. At the time I hadn't understood it.

Now, I thought that she had been a fool to ever stop.

"Belimai?"

I was a third of the way through the bottle when I heard Harper's voice.

I turned too quickly and almost looked right past him.

He looked as tired as ever, but he wasn't wearing his uniform. Instead, he had on a collarless work shirt and dark gray pants. He looked thinner than I remembered, and more pale. The strangest thing about his appearance was that his hands were bare.

"I'd offer to buy you a drink, but you seem to be well ahead of me," Harper said when I just continued staring at his hands.

I drew back slightly and studied Harper without responding. I had no idea what he was doing dressed like this.

"Would you mind if I joined you?" he asked.

"You can do as you please," I said.

"Good enough." He took the chair across from me and poured himself a shot of my gin without asking.

"I didn't think you'd be up and about so soon," he said.

"Apparently I'm harder to kill than you'd think."

Harper frowned and took another shot of gin.

"I didn't think Scott-Beck would go after you." He rolled the empty shot glass between his fingers. "I'm sorry to have done that to you, Belimai."

"It was what you paid me for." I hated the way my skin pricked when he said my name in that quiet, rough tone. I hated the fact that just an offering of a few words could make me want to forgive him.

"So, how is Mr. Talbott taking all this?" I asked, just to get off the subject.

"He's pretty broken up."

"Did you tell him the truth?" I asked.

"It wasn't mine to tell," Harper said. "Do you know what I mean?"

"I think I do, yes." I poured myself a shot and filled Harper's glass also. "It was your stepfather's secret, then Joan's. It wasn't your right to tell it to anyone." I had felt the same way about Sariel. No matter how small of a secret I had been trusted with, I had not wanted to betray it.

But, of course, I had. Harper had not.

"So, where have you been these past few weeks?" I asked.

"In questioning." Harper shook his head. "My abbot wasn't terribly happy with my ignorance as to who shot Mr. Lewis Brown and Mr. Timothy Howard. Nor was he pleased with the fact that I didn't recall your name or description."

"They didn't put you under a prayer engine?"

"No," Harper said quickly. "God, no. If they had, I don't think I could have kept my mouth shut. It was bad enough standing around naked and answering questions for days on end."

"So, what did you say?" I asked.

"I had a surprisingly poor memory of the entire matter." He smiled, but in a bitter way. "The abbot dropped the whole thing once I brought up Scott-Beck's access to Peter Roffcale while he was in custody." Harper took another shot of gin. "We finally reached the understanding that as long as I don't investigate Scott-Beck's life, the abbot won't pursue further questioning of his death."

"So, we all keep our secrets."

"For the time being." Harper ran his bare hand through his hair.

"Are these the clothes they gave you on your release?" I had thought they looked familiar.

"Indeed." Harper touched the front of his rough work shirt. "The very finest in custody-release apparel."

"So, you came straight to the bar?" I smirked.

"No." Harper glanced down as if he were slightly embarrassed. "I went to your apartments. But you weren't home, so I came here."

"Did you think I'd be here, or were you just hoping to drown your sorrow after missing me?"

"That's an interesting question," Harper responded, and then didn't answer it.

I smiled.

"So, why did you want to find me?" I asked.

Harper eyed the bottle of gin and my shot glass.

"I was thinking that I might want to get drunk with you again," he said at last.

There was a moment, as I thought briefly of all that Sariel and I had done to each other, when I could have said no, and that would have been the end of it. But I had grown tired of having only the darkness to keep me company through the night. The gin bottle was still half-full.

I filled Harper's glass and then my own.

Book Two

Captain Harper and the Sixty Second Circle

Chapter One
Rain

*T*he sky was black and pissing rain. On every street, gutters backed up and overflowed. Water gushed over the flagstone walkways and transformed the packed dirt roads into thick rivers of mud.

The gas streetlamp across from Harper spit as rainwater poured in through its cracked housing, flooding the flame. With a loud snap, the safety valve shut the gas line off. The lamp went dark, and the rain continued to pour into the dim, autumn twilight.

Harper hunched under the eaves of the Chapel carriage house. He and three other men had relinquished their seats indoors for a chance to smoke and to escape a cluster of loud schoolgirls who had taken shelter inside. Water soaked into Harper's left sock through a crack in the heel of his boot. The animal odor of wet wool emanated from his black Inquisition coat. Harper pulled his cap a little lower.

He didn't like waiting, particularly not for a carriage that he had no real desire to take. It wasn't pleasure so much as habit and obligation that drew him back to his family estate once every year. The Foster Estate was his only connection to his natural father. It should have meant something to him. Instead, he found himself searching for reasons not to go.

The decision to stay in the capital would have been easy if Belimai had asked him not to go, but he hadn't.

Harper took another drag of his cigarette. It was the last one he had on him. The rest were packed away in his luggage. He closed his eyes and savored the warm smoke.

Beside him, Acolyte Stewarts dragged at his own cigarette and attempted to draw Harper into a conversation. Stewarts smiled a little too hard every time Harper paid him much attention. It made

Harper uncomfortable and added to his desire to abandon the carriage house. Stewarts was only a year or so from becoming quite handsome, and his worshipful exuberance could easily mislead a susceptible man. Harper had no desire to be that man.

"Our first day of vacation, and it's raining like the Great Flood. I'll have to spend the entire time trapped indoors with my wretched Aunt Lucy." Stewarts wiped hopelessly at the water cascading off the brim of his cap and down his nose.

Harper suspected that Stewarts was only moments from asking if he could accompany Harper to his estate house. Stewarts had been flirting with the subject for the last few days. Harper had avoided extending any invitation thus far, but Stewarts possessed a relentless optimism.

The soothing rhythm of falling rain filled the silence between them. Distantly, Harper heard something like the shriek of a bird. He caught it again, but Stewarts' voice broke into his concentration.

"Do you know what I think?" Stewarts asked, and then went on despite Harper's silence. "I think that it would be thrilling to get outside the capital for a vacation. Perhaps go hunting or riding with another fellow. You know, just men."

Harper took advantage of the strange noise to ignore Stewarts. He cocked his head slightly and concentrated on picking it out from the rain again. The violent spattering of rain against the stone walkways and brick houses made a sound like miles of sizzling bacon. Harper leaned out from the cover of the carriage house. He was sure he heard a distant voice calling.

"Abbot Greeley said that you have an estate house north of St. Bennet's Park. That must be nice." Stewarts waited for Harper's response. Then after a moment, he seemed to notice that Harper's attention lay elsewhere. Stewarts surveyed the dim street. The pouring rain covered the normal noises of the street with a fast, crackling patter. Then, suddenly, a high-pitched cry rose out from the noise of the storm.

"A girl probably fell in the mud," Stewarts decided.

"I'd better go see," Harper said.

He stepped out from the cover of the carriage house and started up the street.

"Captain!" Stewarts called after him. "Should I come with you?"

"No. Enjoy your vacation. If I miss the carriage, send my luggage ahead!" Harper shouted back.

He didn't look back to see Stewarts' expression of disappointment. Stewarts, the annoyance of the weather, and even Belimai's indifference to his departure no longer troubled Harper. He poured his concentration into finding the woman.

Mud and filthy water splashed up around his calves and sucked at his boots as he rushed through the open street and crossed to the cobblestone walkway. He only paused to listen, and then he raced on. He could hear the woman's voice clearly now.

"Please, someone help! He's going to kill her! God, please!" Her voice broke with a sob. A loud burst of thunder swallowed her further cries.

Harper sprinted after the sound of the woman's voice. He searched the lines of stately houses, iron-worked gates, and flowering hedges for any sight of her. The walkways were empty. Rain and darkness had driven most people indoors.

Harper noticed a motion, a dim white form almost buried in the mud of the street. She pulled herself up to her feet and stumbled forward.

"Please, help." Her voice broke in ragged exhaustion.

Harper reached her in a moment.

"Thank God," she moaned as she saw his Inquisitor's coat and emblems.

She staggered to him. For a moment, Harper simply supported her frail body. Her white serving dress sagged with rain and mud. The filthy hem of her petticoat tangled around her legs. Harper felt tremors of exhaustion shudder through her legs as she leaned against him.

"Are you all right?" Harper asked.

"It's Miss Leticia. You have to help her." The old woman collapsed against Harper. He lifted her easily and carried her to shelter. He lowered her to a decorative bench beneath an iron gateway. The surrounding boxwood hedge offered them a little cover from the rain.

"Please," she whispered to him, "help Miss Leticia."

"Where is she?" Harper knew better than to question the old woman further.

"The Rose House. 834." The old woman closed her eyes as tears began to flood down her creased cheeks. "He's going to kill her this time. I know he is."

"834. North or South Chapel?" Harper asked quickly.

"North," she whispered. "Please hurry."

"I will." Harper took off running. After two blocks, Chapel Street forked into north and south branches. Harper sprinted up the north branch. The houses grew steadily more opulent, and the gates more formidable. He ran another four blocks before reaching the addresses in the 800s.

Harper didn't know how long the old woman had been staggering down the street calling for help. He silently prayed that it had been a matter of minutes rather than hours. Harper ran with all his strength, knowing that no matter how quickly he went, time was not on his side. Wounds were inflicted in moments; lives could be taken in a matter of seconds.

When Harper reached the elegant marble gate of 834, he expected that he might have to climb it. To his surprise, he found it unlocked. It seemed wrong that the gate should be left open, but he did not stop to think about it. He sprinted past the line of curling willows, took the stone stairs to the house two at a time, and at last stopped in front of the entry doors. Light radiated from the windows on the first floor, but only two windows on the second floor were illuminated. Harper slammed the polished brass knocker against the wood with a resounding blow.

A well-dressed servant opened the door immediately. He looked pale and deeply unhappy. He glanced at the silver Inquisition emblems on Harper's collar and quickly stepped aside to allow Harper in.

"Thank you for coming so quickly, Captain," he murmured.

"Should I take you up to Miss Let...to the body?" The man looked horrified at the words that had come out of his mouth.

"I can show myself up." Harper felt a change in himself the moment he knew the woman was dead. The pounding blood in his veins and his racing heart all suddenly went flat. The moment when he might have arrived in time to save the woman had passed. His passion and hope cut off like the gas in the safety valve of a streetlamp.

"Which room is she in?" Harper asked.

"I don't know. I haven't been up. They...She...I don't know, sir." The doorman flushed, clearly unsure of how to treat Harper, or how to even address the body upstairs. No rules of etiquette dictated polite behavior in the wake of a murder. The doorman foundered into a series of apologies. Harper was accustomed to such awkwardness and carried on.

"That's fine," Harper said. "I'll find it."

A staircase dominated the entryway. It rose in a majestic curve of marble and highly polished brass. Harper strode up the steps. He was used to having full run of other people's homes during the first paralyzed hours after a crime. He took in the house as he went up. The floor was laid out in a checkerboard of white and rose marble. Light gleamed from crystal chandeliers and glinted across the gilded scrolls that decorated the wallpaper.

A few steps from the second floor, Harper stopped. The stairs ahead of him were wet and smelled of soap. Someone had washed this section of the staircase less than an hour ago. Harper went up more slowly, checking each step before he set his muddy boots on it.

Deep in the groove, where the brass railing met the pale marble stairs, was a thin line of bright red blood. Several long black hairs were caught there also. Harper noted the length of the hairs, then continued.

The staircase opened into a wide hallway. Six tall doors lined both walls of the hallway. Light glowed from beneath two of the closest doors on the right. Harper noticed a few more spots on the floor where the marble shone wetly from a recent cleaning.

As he moved closer, Harper heard the voices of two men coming from behind the farther of the two doors. The men spoke in hushed tones, and Harper couldn't clearly distinguish their words. He unbuttoned his overcoat to allow himself easy access to his pistol. Then he started down the hall.

He stopped, noticing that the signs of cleaning ended at the first door. Harper nudged the door open.

It was clearly a girl's bedroom. The rug, the wallpaper, the swaying curtains, and even the big canopy bed were all white. A pattern of gold and pale pink roses covered the carpet. White lace dripped over the edge of the dressing table. The bed billowed up from the rest of the room like a wedding cake in a bakery window.

Harper stepped into the room slowly, studying each foot of floor before marking it with his filthy boots. Blots of vivid red led him from the door to the far side of the bed.

The girl lay on her side. A pool of blood formed a dark red halo around her head. Harper crouched down beside her. The entire back of her skull was a mat of black hair, blood, and jutting bone.

Her neck hung awkwardly between her cracked skull and shoulders. As Harper looked over her body, he noticed old yellow bruises beneath newer blue ones. When he pulled aside the white sleeve of her nightgown, he found that the marks were still red, the bruises not yet darkened.

From the old woman's words, Harper knew that a man had been beating the girl. From the marks on her body, it was obvious that the beatings had been going on for quite a while. Perhaps the girl had attempted to escape and fallen down the stairs. Or possibly the man had thrown her down.

Harper guessed what the men in the other room whispered about so urgently. They could clean up the stairs and hall, but they couldn't wash away the broken bone and deep bruises on the dead girl's body. Harper decided that it was time to talk to them.

Harper stood to leave when he noticed that he had made a mistake upon entering the room. He had thought the glass doors to the girl's balcony had been open. Now, as the curtains fluttered in the storm wind, he saw that the doors were still closed. The glass had been broken out. Harper checked for any shards of glass on the white rug. There were none.

He stepped out onto the balcony. It was too dark to see clearly, and the rainwater hid the glitter that the broken glass would have given off. Harper moved his gloved hands through the water, feeling for the hard edges of glass. He found dozens of shards in just a few moments.

"She's in here," he heard a man say, and then the door to the girl's room swung wide. As Harper watched from the dark balcony, three men entered the room. Harper recognized the first two from the Brighton Inquisition: Captain Brandson and Abbot Greeley. A man in a dark violet dressing gown followed after them.

Brandson's pale face was spattered with orange freckles, and his black coat, like Harper's own, was soaking from the rain. Brandson's fine red hair dribbled water down his face. He had clearly left his cap behind when he had been called to the murder. It was like Brandson to forget something like that.

The abbot's thick shock of white hair was perfectly dry. Despite his age, he looked much more fit than Brandson. He gestured to the dead girl's body offhandedly, as if she were a curiosity he had already seen.

The third man Harper did not know, but his face seemed familiar. He was in his late forties, a few years younger than the abbot. His black hair was streaked with gray and swept back in a rather handsome manner. The elegance of his tall, slim form almost allowed Harper overlook the white bandage wrapped around his right hand. As if sensing Harper's eyes on him, he hid his hand in the pocket of his dressing gown.

"As you can see…" Abbot Greeley directed Brandson's gaze. "The intruder broke in through the glass doors there and attacked her while she was preparing for bed—"

"I don't think that was the case."

The three other men jumped at the sound of Harper's voice. He stepped in from the balcony.

"Captain Harper." A flush of anger colored Abbot Greeley's tanned face. "What in the name of God are you doing here?"

Even at the best of times, a deep, mutual hostility seethed between Harper and Abbot Greeley. Because the abbot was his superior, Harper masked his animosity with expressionless professionalism. As a rule, the abbot did the same. For five years they had maintained that tenuous illusion of civility. But since Peter Roffcale's murder, even that had begun to collapse.

"Investigating a murder, sir," Harper replied.

"You were given vacation leave four hours ago," Abbot Greeley snapped. "You shouldn't even be in town."

Harper realized that the abbot's voice had been one of the two he had heard whispering in the other room. Harper wondered how long Abbot Greeley had been at the crime scene. Certainly long enough for his clothes and hair to dry, despite the soaking rain outside.

"I heard a woman on the street calling for help. She sent me here to try and reach the girl before she was killed." Harper held the accusation back from his voice. "May I ask how you happen to be here, sir? Normally you'd be at home by this hour, wouldn't you?"

"Lord Cedric and I are good friends." Abbot Greeley gestured to the man in the violet dressing robe. "He sent for me the moment he saw what had befallen his poor niece."

"You have my condolences, sir." Harper had seen photographs of Lord Cedric in the social columns of the papers. He recalled that the man was a cousin to the bishop of Redstone, but little else.

"Thank you," Lord Cedric said quietly. Harper recognized the rich depth of his voice. He had been the second man up in the room with Abbot Greeley.

Clearly, Lord Cedric had sent for the abbot long before he had called for any Inquisitors. The abbot would have instructed Lord Cedric in the matter of erasing evidence. It wouldn't have taken long to move the girl's body from the stairs to her bedroom and hide the signs of her previous beatings under a long nightgown. A maid would be called to clean the stairs and hall. Then, to concoct a murderous intruder, they smashed the glass doors. Their deception had been created in haste, and no doubt Abbot Greeley knew that any decent investigator would have seen through it.

But then Abbot Greeley had the advantage of choosing which Inquisition captain to summon. Briefly, Harper glanced at Brandson. The captain flipped his wet hair back from his face. He picked up one of the dead girl's hairbrushes, considered it for a moment, and then, noticing Harper's gaze, returned it to the dressing table.

"Good of you to come, Harper," Abbot Greeley said. "But we have things well in hand now. You can get back to your vacation."

"I'd be happy to." Harper continued to study Brandson. He'd never thought highly of the captain's intellect, but perhaps he could be roused to thought. "Before I go, however, I can't help but wonder what's become of the footprints and water from the intruder?"

"Well." Brandson pointed to Harper's own tracks. "Those would be them, I would say."

"I'm afraid I have a pretty tight alibi, Brandson." Harper crossed his arms over his chest. "Those are from my boots. Moreover, they don't lead in from the balcony to the body. There aren't any tracks leading in from the balcony."

"That's impossible. A rug this white would have been marked. No one could break in and not leave a single print." Brandson frowned down at the white carpet.

"A Prodigal could. One of the flyers wouldn't need to set foot on the floor." Abbot Greeley offered Harper an angry smile. "Thank you for pointing that out, Captain Harper. We now know that we are looking for a Prodigal."

"Shouldn't you also consider the possibility that no one broke in?" Harper directed the question to Brandson. "Someone might have shattered the glass to make it look like there had been an intruder—"

Abbot Greeley cut Harper off. "Captain Brandson can certainly draw his own conclusions, Harper." He still smiled at Harper, but his eyes were narrowed in anger. "I'm sure we've kept you from your vacation long enough. Brandson and I will take care of things here."

"Of course. I should be going then," Harper stated coldly.

"What about the maid?" Lord Cedric's voice carried from behind Brandson and Greeley.

Abbot Greeley glanced back at Lord Cedric, then to Harper.

"Quite right. Harper, where is the woman who sent you here? We'll need to speak to her."

Harper had no intention of handing the old woman over to Abbot Greeley, not after what had happened to Peter Roffcale. At the same time, he didn't have the proof or the authority to outrightly challenge the abbot. The woman hadn't actually accused Lord Cedric by name. All Harper had was his own conviction, and that wouldn't stand up against the abbot's authority.

"I left her at the Convent of the Pierced Heart." Harper picked the most plausible place in the vicinity. Pierced Heart had the added advantage of being farthest from where he had actually left the old woman. Harper wasn't sure if Abbot Greeley believed him, but it didn't matter. All that mattered was that he answered. So long as Harper didn't directly disobey orders, the abbot couldn't have him locked up or discharged.

"Right, then," Brandson said. "I'll send two of my men out to take a statement from Captain Harper's witness."

"Send Reynolds and Miller. If they don't find the woman at the convent, have them search north toward the Chapel Street carriage house," Abbot Greeley said.

Brandson nodded.

"Also..." Abbot Greeley gave a quick glance to the shattered glass doors. "Send Camp, Thurston, and Wills out to round up the Prodigal flyers that we have on record. I want a confession from one of them within the next week."

Again Brandson nodded, as if the thought had been his own. The fact that a Prodigal had been designated as the murderer even before the investigation began didn't seem to bother Brandson. Only Abbot Greeley's orders seemed to penetrate his thoughts.

Harper had once wondered how Brandson managed to rise to the rank of captain. He supposed that he was now witnessing the qualities that Abbot Greeley so valued in Brandson.

"With your permission, sir, I think I had better get back to my vacation." Harper inclined his head slightly to the abbot out of habit.

"A very good idea, Captain Harper. I don't want to catch a glimpse of you until you're due back." Abbot Greeley smiled as if he were joking. Harper wondered if the abbot actually thought he was fooling him.

"We can both hope," Harper replied, and then left the house.

Chapter Two
Needle

*T*he old woman hung against Harper like a mass of soaked laundry. She was limp in his arms, her body and limbs buried in the filthy, dripping fabric of her dress. Her wrinkled face was nearly as colorless as her lace cap and white hair. Only the short wisps of her breath brushing against his collar assured Harper that she was even alive.

For a brief moment Harper thought that she had died when he first returned to her, but he found a pulse still weakly throbbing through the pale veins of her wrist. She hadn't awakened when he shook her, only letting out a weak groan. Her skin felt icy and tremors shuddered through her body. She needed to be taken to a physician. He quickly wrapped her in his coat.

She shivered, and Harper pulled her closer to the heat of his own body. Her lace cap hung in a tangle with her hair. One of the little hairpins jabbed into the side of Harper's neck as he walked. He shifted the old woman's unconscious body against his shoulder, and her cap fell entirely free.

Harper knew that he should stop and retrieve the cap. It might take only one scrap of lace to serve as a trail. But time was already against him. He didn't dare stop and fish through the mud while this woman died. He kept walking and hoped that the mud and darkness would hide whatever trail lay behind him. His best chance lay in putting as much distance between himself and the Chapel streets as quickly as possible.

It wouldn't take Reynolds and Miller long to discover that the woman hadn't been left at the Convent of the Pierced Heart. The moment they realized that, they would be hunting. That knowledge gave Harper a rush of strength, and he quickened his step.

Reynolds and Miller worked fast and took a deep pleasure in their searches. As a team, they hunted more like hounds than men. Harper had seen them chase down a murderer on no more of a trail than the print of a boot heel and a whiff of cologne. They hadn't been easy on the man either. They had brought him in with a broken leg and a gash across his hand so deep that it had required sixty stitches. Harper had always enjoyed having them assigned to one of his investigations.

Tonight he wished the two of them had found other occupations.

Harper reached the Brighton and Chapel Street carriage house just as city bells began to toll out the change of the hour. The south carriage would normally have been gone already, but the bad weather had slowed the drive. It arrived just after him. He had to wait with the old woman cradled in his arms for ten minutes while the horses were changed and the driver took a piss in the street.

Inside the shelter of the carriage, Harper allowed himself to relax a little. The old woman no longer shook against him. She lay still, sleeping. Only one other passenger climbed into the carriage after Harper. The young man was wearing a muddy school robe in the colors of St. Christopher's College. He reeked of too much sweet wine. He collapsed into the seat across from Harper, then sat bolt upright.

"Good God, are you here to arrest me?"

"No." Harper stole a glance out the window to see if Miller or Reynolds had gotten this far yet. Two blocks up, beneath one of the few remaining lamps, he thought he caught the outline of an Inquisitor's long coat. The figure was there only a moment and then gone into the darkness.

"I was only having a few sips of sherry to keep off the cold," the young student slurred at Harper. "The carriage was late. Please don't bring me up for Penance."

"Quiet," Harper told him flatly.

The young man pressed his lips together absurdly and squashed himself back into his seat.

Harper kept watching out the small window. Silently he counted the passing seconds to himself. When he had been a boy, he had gotten in the habit of keeping his nerves calm with this steady silent count. As Harper reached the count of eight, he saw Reynolds.

Reynolds was a surprisingly small man with misleadingly youthful features. At the moment, as he stepped swiftly through the shaft of light from a window across the street, he was beaming like a schoolboy.

Harper had counted to ten when Miller appeared. He could have been Reynolds' twin if it hadn't been for his black mustache and slightly darker hair. Miller tossed something limp and partly white to Reynolds. It was the lace cap. The pulse of Harper's blood began to quicken.

Twelve, Harper counted. Reynolds gestured ahead. Miller nodded.

Thirteen. They began to run toward the carriage house.

Fourteen. Harper calmly latched the lock on the nearest door and then reached past the drunken student and locked the opposite door.

Fifteen. Miller was close enough that even through the rain, Harper could see the glint of his little round spectacles beneath his black cap. Reynolds was bounding ahead through the mud as if it were scarcely there.

Sixteen.

Harper was suddenly rocked back into the thin padding of his seat as the carriage pulled out into the street. He kept watching as the carriage rushed farther and farther away from the two Inquisitors. It was only when he had come to a full count of sixty that Harper leaned back against the worn seat of the carriage and relaxed enough to pay any attention to the student across from him. The young man swayed back and forth as he clumsily tried to shove a half-empty bottle of wine under his seat cushion.

Some men certainly hid their deceptions better than others, Harper decided, but he said nothing of it.

At St. Christopher's Park, he lifted the old woman back into his arms and carefully got out of the carriage. Here the houses were not as sprawling as those of Chapel Street, but they stood against the black, storming sky with a conservative elegance. Harper walked quickly, ignoring the tired ache in his back and legs. Four blocks up the line of steepled roofs and miniature rose hedges, Harper reached his destination.

The house had been recently rebuilt, and Harper was no longer familiar with it. There had been six steps to the front door before. Now there were seven, and Harper almost tripped on the last one. It worried him that the woman didn't wake at all when he stumbled. He pulled the bell a little more violently than was necessary and waited.

It was late enough that most of the house staff would have been in bed or gone for the day. Harper jerked the bell chain again. Only a moment later, the door opened.

Edward took a quick look at Harper, then the old woman in his arms, and let them in.

"What happened?" Edward asked as he led Harper past the waiting room and into the consulting room.

"Exposure, I think. She's been out in the cold most of the night."

"Lay her on the table." Edward pushed his blonde hair from his face. One of his cheeks was much redder than the other. Harper guessed that he had fallen asleep at his desk again.

As Harper lay the woman down on the raised nursing table, Edward reached past him and took her pulse. Edward frowned slightly and placed his hand against her pale cold cheek. Gently, Edward brushed Harper aside and stripped the wet black coat off the woman. He tossed it to the floor.

"She collapsed on the street." Harper stepped back out of Edward's way.

There was a chair, but he felt too agitated to sit. He hung behind Edward waiting for something to do. Edward pulled the old woman's eyes open, then let the lids drop back closed. Then, carefully, Edward ran his fingers along the woman's neck and over her head.

Harper wanted to pace, but the room was too small, and he knew he'd just get in Edward's way. He wasn't good at waiting while another man took care of things. He had to keep himself from restlessly picking up the surgical instruments in the room and toying with them.

"Will she be all right?" Harper asked.

"I think so...It doesn't look like she hurt her head when she fell. Her neck feels fine as well. These clothes have to go." With a practiced ease, Edward grabbed a pair of surgical scissors and sliced off the filthy remains of the woman's clothes. He studied her withered white body for a moment.

"Her knee looks bad. It'll need stitches." Edward moved quickly past Harper, gathering the supplies he would need. "There aren't any swellings from broken bones that I can see. Aside from her knee and the cold, she seems just fine." He paused a moment to catch Harper's eye. "By the way, it's good to see you at last."

Harper nodded and tried not to look awkward. In the last two months he had hardly seen Edward at all. He knew he should have been there to comfort Edward after Joan's funeral. But pretending to mourn while Edward truly suffered made Harper feel sick with his own deception.

It had been easier to bury himself in work and avoid all thoughts of the matter.

"I've been busy...I'm sorry." Harper offered the excuse flatly.

"I understand. I've been trying to keep myself busy too." Edward filled a basin and rinsed his hands. "Will you be going out to the Foster Estate again this year?"

"I was on my way when I came across this woman."

Edward nodded.

"Do you think you might have a few days free after that?" he asked.

"I wasn't thinking of staying there the entire month," Harper said. "Just a week or so. After that I'll be free. Why don't we plan on getting together next week?"

"I'd really like that." Edward smiled brightly for a moment, then his attention returned to the old woman.

"Older ladies shouldn't be hauled around through storms, you know? You should have sent for me. It would have been just as fast for me to come to you as it was for you to get her here to me."

"I'll remember that next time," Harper replied.

"No, you won't." Edward smiled. "You couldn't stand to just wait around for me to get to you."

As he spoke, Edward sponged the mud and water off her and then covered her with a thick cotton blanket. He left only her wounded, right leg exposed.

Harper watched as Edward laid out the tools he would need: the long curving needles, silk thread, gauze, a hypodermic needle and syringe. Harper stared at the syringe for a moment as a feeling of dread welled up through him.

"Belimai," Harper whispered, and Edward glanced up to him.

"What?" Edward asked.

"Edward, I have to go." Harper started for the door.

"What about this woman?" Edward demanded.

"I'll be back for her. Just don't let anyone know she's here with you, all right? Especially not anyone from the Inquisition." Harper knew he was asking more of Edward than he had a right to, but he had no other choice. "I have to go. They may kill him if I don't get to him first."

"Wait! Will, who are you talking about?"

"I'll explain later."

Harper bolted out, leaving his coat behind. All he could think of was that time was not with him tonight. No matter how fast he ran, no matter how brutally he forced strength into his exhausted body, the moments between life and death slipped past him.

Chapter Three
Black Nails

*T*he rain worsened, and the packed dirt of the streets softened into a citywide bog. Harper ran hard, keeping to the raised walkways. In the street beside him, cart horses struggled to pull themselves and their burdens through the thick mud. Harper crossed the road at Butcher Street. He sank almost to his knees. The mud clung to Harper's legs and pulled at him as he fought his way forward.

Frigid rain slapped down against him. His wet clothes clung to his body, spreading the chill of wind and rain across his skin. Mud oozed through the crack in his boot heel. If he had thought about it, Harper might have noticed that he could hardly feel his fingers or toes anymore.

But he didn't think about it. Just as he didn't think of what the Inquisition men could have done if they had already found Belimai. Vivid, bleeding images flickered through Harper's mind, but he did not acknowledge them.

He counted silently to mute the fear surging through him. It was easier to count the moments that passed than to think of what could occur during them. After sixty he began again at one, turning time back on itself in a sixty second circle. As he had once named devils so that they could have no power over him, he now named the seconds. Another man might have prayed, but Harper had abandoned prayer long ago.

Harper's darkest fears, those that hunted him even in his dreams, were bred from this constant, hopeless race. In his nightmares, he always arrived too late. No matter how hard he ran, moments slipped past him. He reached his mother only an instant after her death. He burst into his stepfather's study to find his pipe still burning but the man gone, never to return. He never even came close to reaching his sister before her tears turned to streams of furious blood.

Harper rounded the corner of Butcher Street and sprinted toward the slumping, three-story tenement where Belimai lived. Harper took the stairs up to Belimai's rented rooms in quick leaps. At the top of the staircase, all of his driving energy slammed to a halt. Belimai's door hung crookedly off its hinges. The doorjamb had been reduced to a shattered mass of splinters.

Past the broken door, Harper glimpsed the wreckage of Belimai's home. The walls were stripped bare. All of the books lay in heaps among pieces of smashed furniture and slashed upholstery. A wide spill of ink bled out from the cracked body of Belimai's desk. Sheaves of Belimai's drawings were strewn everywhere. A delicate sketch of a grasshopper lay on the floor near Harper. The paper was crumpled and marked with the muddy impression of a boot heel.

Suddenly Harper was aware of the rawness of his throat. Sharp, biting pain lanced through his chest. His legs trembled, and for a moment he didn't know if he could remain standing. He closed his eyes and leaned against the hard support of the doorframe.

Then, from inside the room, he heard a softly whispered obscenity.

Harper shoved the door open in time to catch Belimai climbing back in through one of the shattered windows. For an instant Harper felt the overwhelming urge to rush forward and pull Belimai to him. Belimai's expression stopped him. Belimai's pale yellow eyes were slitted with fury, his thin lips drawn back in a hiss of rage. Harper froze, giving Belimai a moment to recognize him. Belimai didn't quite smile, but the fear and anger drained from his expression.

The kinky branches of Belimai's black hair hung dripping around his bare shoulders. He wore only a pair of wet, black pants and a single sock. He folded his thin arms over his chest, surveying the ruins of his home.

"You just missed your friends." Belimai went to his desk and began searching through its broken hull.

"They're likely to come back." Harper wanted to offer some comfort, but he knew that Belimai wouldn't accept it. There was some deep perversity about Belimai that made him despise kindness. He avoided compliments as if they were collection notices. Sympathy simply made him furious.

"I thought you were supposed to be at some country estate this week." Belimai jerked at the crumpled desk drawers. The jammed pieces of wood resisted him.

"I missed my carriage," Harper replied.

"I guess it's been a bad day all around then." Belimai continued prying at the drawer. He finally clawed off the drawer face with his long black nails.

"Those fucking bastards." Belimai lifted out the cracked bodies of several glass syringes as if they had been cherished pets.

"Bastards." Belimai glared at the shattered needles before he hurled them aside.

"We need to go," Harper reminded Belimai. "They probably only left to ask your neighbors if they know where you are. They'll be back. It's standard procedure."

"Standard procedure for what?" Belimai looked up at Harper. "Did I break some arcane law by putting pictures on the walls? Why the hell did they do this?" Belimai swept his pale arms out over the wreckage littering his floor.

"A lord's niece was murdered this evening. You're one of the suspects." At first Harper wasn't sure if Belimai understood him. Belimai said nothing. He simply sat staring at the huge spill of ink in front of him. Then Belimai stood and walked to the bedroom. Harper heard him rifling through his broken belongings and cursing very softly.

Harper watched the stairs. Now that he wasn't running, he felt the cold sinking through his wet uniform. He wondered if Belimai was ever going to come out of the bedroom.

If it were Edward in there, Harper would have simply followed him into the room and seen what he was doing. If he were packing, Harper would have helped him. If he were crying and cursing his luck, then Harper would have told him to do it later.

But Belimai was not at all like Edward. Belimai was deeply private. Even when Harper held Belimai's naked body against his own, touching and exploring every inch of him, he wasn't sure of his right to ask if it pleased Belimai. Physically, he knew Belimai well. But beyond the flesh, Harper knew less of Belimai's feelings than did the fleas in Belimai's bed.

Harper was scratching his shoulder involuntarily at the thought of fleas when Belimai emerged from his bedroom. He had dressed and held a satchel of belongings. His wet hair was tucked under a black cap that Harper was almost positive had once been his. Belimai offered Harper an ugly green coat and a pair of gloves.

The coat didn't do much to warm Harper's wet body, but it kept the wind from chilling him further.

"You left those gloves last time you were here," Belimai said. Harper removed his wet gloves and stuffed them into his pocket before pulling on the dry pair.

"I thought you said that you couldn't find them." Harper flexed his fingers against the tight leather.

"I did say that, didn't I?" Belimai shrugged. "Shall we go?"

"Do you have everything you need?" Harper didn't want to delay, but more than that, he didn't want to have to come back.

"I've got what I can carry. That will have to be enough, won't it?" Belimai's pale yellow eyes flickered over the ruined belongings that he was leaving behind.

"Let's go, then." Harper held the door for Belimai and felt absurd doing it. Belimai seemed too depressed to even offer a snide comment.

Harper followed Belimai through narrow alleys of tenements and workhouses. Eruptions of low thunder rolled through the noise of heavy machinery. Steam spewed out of chimneys only to be beaten down by the pelting rain. Most of the gas lamps had gone out, but distant flickers of lightning lit the sky from time to time.

As they walked steadily onward, the smell of the river began to drift through the rain and wind. They passed the cannery row and threaded their way between the lines of massive water pumps and sewage pipes.

At last, Belimai stopped beside the abandoned remains of a beached trawler. He pushed aside a sheet of corroded metal and started into the darkness of the ship's decrepit hull. The smell of urine and rotting kelp wafted out of the opening. Harper noticed the shadows of people watching them from inside the trawler's hull. Most of them had yellow eyes, like Belimai.

Harper caught Belimai's arm.

"This is where you're planning to stay?" Harper asked.

"It's out of the rain," Belimai replied.

"It's a shit hole." At the best of times, Harper found Belimai's living conditions a little too run down, but this was actually revolting.

"I'm not planning to move in," Belimai replied. "The Crone does her recruiting here."

"The Butcher Street Crone?" Harper lowered his voice as several of the Prodigals inside the boat stared at him. All of them were likely to be fugitives like Belimai, who were willing to work as whores and cutthroats in exchange for the Crone's protection from the Inquisition.

"Are you seriously thinking of working for the Crone?" Harper tightened his grip on Belimai's thin arm. "At best she'll make a whore of you. More likely she'll have you murdering honest men for ophorium."

"It might save me the trouble of buying the drug myself," Belimai responded.

A burning pain flared up through Harper's chest at the thought of Belimai ending up gutted on an Inquisition table or screaming from an execution fire. Even the Butcher Boys who weren't executed might as well have died. They were vacant bodies, living only to feed their addictions.

"She'll only use you, Belimai. As soon as you're too worn out or old, she'll let the Inquisition have you," Harper said.

"I worked for the Crone after I was first released from the Inquisition. She took good care of me then." Belimai's tone was oddly flat. "I'm accused of murdering a lord's niece. The Inquisition isn't going to just stop looking for me, and I can't hide in the clouds for the rest of my life. But the Crone has connections. If anyone can get a Prodigal out of the capital, she can. I'll just have to do a couple jobs for her first. Nothing I haven't done before." Belimai pulled free of Harper's grip. He gave Harper a short, forced smile.

"I guess we should call this goodbye—" Belimai began.

"Like hell." Harper grabbed Belimai at the waist and flung him up over his shoulder. Then he turned with Belimai and walked away from the rotting ship.

"Harper." Belimai hung limply against Harper's back. "What do you think you're doing?"

"What I damn well should have done from the start," Harper snapped. "I didn't run myself half to death just to hand you over to the Butcher Street Crone. I came to save your life, and no matter what you want, that's what I'm going to do."

"Harper, if you're caught with me—"

"Shut up." Harper didn't want to hear why he shouldn't be doing what he was doing. He knew the reasons well enough.

"At least put me down," Belimai demanded. "If anything is going to make an Inquisitor notice us, this is it."

"You are not going to work for the Crone," Harper stated flatly.

"All right. Just let me down."

Harper decided to oblige Belimai, partly because they looked conspicuous, but mainly because he was too tired to carry Belimai any farther. Harper set Belimai on his feet and then leaned back against a cannery wall. The slight overhang of its roof sheltered him from the rain. Belimai joined him against the wall.

"If you're found out helping me, they'll skin you alive," Belimai said.

"I'm thinking," Harper replied. He stared out at the sky.

He couldn't just take Belimai back to his house. His upstanding neighbors would report it in a matter of hours. Belimai would be safest outside the city, but every road and pier had checkpoints. The normal security would be intensified after a murder. Even Prodigals with special passes to leave the capital would be held back tonight. By morning, word would have spread, and even the lax security allowed for wealthy travelers would be tightened.

He wished he had a cigarette and dry feet.

"If this damn rain just would let up…" Harper muttered, as if all their troubles could be blamed on the weather.

"It's worse up high." Belimai gazed up into the dark clouds. Reflections of bursting lightning flickered across his yellow eyes.

"Is that where you went when they broke in your door?"

"Of course. As soon as I heard the wood crack, I was out the window. With the weather like this, there was no chance they could catch me in a net." Belimai frowned slightly. "But even I can't stay up there all the time. I nearly froze."

Harper considered hiding Belimai in Hells Below. Joan would take Belimai if Harper asked her to, he was sure of that. She might have changed her name, but she was still Harper's sister. But Hells Below was the first place anyone would look for a fugitive Prodigal. Also, Nick Sariel was there. Harper didn't like the idea of Belimai and Nick becoming reacquainted. Harper gazed at Belimai's sharp features. No, he didn't like the thought of Belimai and Sariel living together in Good Commons at all.

"That is my cap you're wearing, isn't it?" Harper asked.

"You left it after that first night you spent with me." Belimai pushed the brim up a little so that it didn't cover so much of his face. "I thought it would be best if they didn't find any of your things in my rooms."

"Smart." Harper stepped back from Belimai, studying his slim figure. The rain had soaked Belimai's navy coat to black. Between that and the cap, he could have been mistaken for an Inquisitor. No one catching sight of his black fingernails or yellow eyes would be fooled, but there were ways of hiding both.

"Should I ask what you're planning?" Belimai inquired.

"That would ruin the surprise," Harper replied. "Hold this, will you?"

Harper pulled off his coat and handed it to Belimai. The wind sliced through Harper's wet clothes and sent shivers rushing over his skin. Quickly he unbuttoned his uniform jacket and peeled it off. He handed it to Belimai.

"Is this a plan that involves us warming each other with our naked bodies?" Belimai gave Harper a lewd smile.

"Maybe later." Harper unclipped his stiff priest's collar and then fitted it around Belimai's throat.

Belimai arched a black brow at him.

"Now, put on my uniform jacket," Harper said.

"You have to be joking," Belimai said.

"I'm not," Harper replied.

Belimai shrugged and put on Harper's jacket. It wasn't a perfect fit, but the dark coat disguised the discrepancies. Belimai's thin frame became a solid black form from which the two silver Inquisitor's emblems and the white priest's collar stood out sharply.

"You almost look good enough to salute." Harper took his heavy green coat back from Belimai and put it on quickly.

"What about these?" Belimai held up his hands. His black nails caught the light of a distant gas lamp like obsidian.

"Gloves." Harper began peeling his off. "They worked for my sister and stepfather for years; there's no reason they shouldn't work for you."

"Just a minute." Belimai pulled a jack knife out of his boot and flipped the blade open. Instinctively, Harper flinched. It had nothing to do with Belimai; only the speed of his movement and the razor edge of the knife blade.

Belimai sliced through the curve of his thumbnail and then continued cutting the rest of his nails down to the tips of his fingers. The knife only slipped once when a tremor passed through Belimai's hand. The blade sank down into the side of his finger and bright red blood welled up.

"Fuck," Belimai snarled.

"Is it bad?" Harper caught Belimai's hand to inspect the cut.

"No," Belimai replied. "I'm just starting to get the shakes."

"You should've had me do it." Harper squeezed the cut, trying to stop the bleeding. Belimai hissed at him.

"What are you doing?"

"Stopping the bleeding. You apply pressure," Harper said.

"What kind of cretin are you? Haven't you ever heard of kissing it and making it better?"

"You have to be joking," Harper replied.

"No, it works. You put it in your mouth and suck on it."

"I thought only children did that." Harper started to laugh, then noticed Belimai's narrowed eyes. "All right then, I'll do it if you'd like."

He pressed his lips against Belimai's finger and then gently kissed the small cut. A little of Belimai's blood slipped between his lips.

It was hot and tasted sharp, as if it had been mixed with wine. As he swallowed, Harper felt a burning trail slide down his throat. Heat flooded his stomach and sank deep into his groin. It washed outward through the muscles of his arms and legs.

Harper drew in a breath of the cold air. The scents of fish and cats, of machine grease and his own pungent sweat, rolled through his lungs. He felt currents of wind twist and flow over him as if they were ribbons that he could catch in his hands.

He stepped back from Belimai, but already the sensation was fading. A moment later all that remained was a slight warmth in the pit of his stomach.

"Is something wrong?" Belimai asked.

"No." Harper should have known better than to taste Belimai's blood.

"Just put these on." Harper handed Belimai his gloves.

"You're sure—"

"Your eyes are still too easy to see." Harper pulled the cap lower over Belimai's face. The shadow of the brim fell well below Belimai's eyes. "There. Perfect."

"So, now what?" Belimai asked.

"We walk down to the Green-Hill carriage house and take the last carriage out to St. Bennet's."

"Are you insane?" Belimai stared at him. "If there's been a murder, the Inquisition will have men staking out every carriage house, dock, and city gate."

"They will be looking for Prodigals, not other Inquisitors. When they ask your name, you tell them William J. Harper—"

"I'm going to claim to be you? That will never work."

"It will work just fine. Trust me."

"What if they ask me what the 'J' stands for?" Belimai asked.

"They aren't going to ask—"

"I think I ought to know," Belimai snapped. "If I'm claiming to be William J. Harper, then I want to know what the 'J' stands for."

"Jubal," Harper said at last.

"Jubal?" Belimai cocked his head slightly. "What kind of name is that?"

"Jubal, son of Lamech and Adah. 'Father of all such as handle the harp and organ.' Genesis 4:21."

"So, they knew when you were born that you'd be an organ handler?" Belimai smirked.

"And aren't you glad they were right?" Harper replied. He was relieved to see Belimai smile slightly in response.

"Don't you think that they'll know I'm not you?" Belimai asked.

"They won't know if we go to Archer's Green. I've never been there, and none of their courthouses overlap with ours in Brighton. Someone might recognize my name, but that's all," Harper said. "We'll wait until the carriage has pulled up, then we'll walk in and give our names and destinations. We'll pay and get in the carriage, and that will be that. There won't be time for any small talk with the other Inquisitors. All right?"

Belimai took in a deep breath and then exhaled slowly. Harper noticed the slight tremors that passed through Belimai's body. For the first time in their acquaintance, Harper wished that he had a few grams of ophorium to offer Belimai, just to still his shaking. Belimai shoved his trembling hands into his coat pockets.

"I suppose that I'll just pretend that all this shaking is from the cold. You think they'll believe that at the carriage house?"

"No one will even ask," Harper replied.

"What if they do? What if they take one look at me and know I'm not you?"

"Then we'll just run like hell." Harper gripped Belimai's shoulder and stepped back out into the rain with him. "Come on. Everything will be fine."

"Oh, yes. How could we fail with such a foolproof plan? You're really wasting your talents in the Inquisition, you know. You ought to work for the war department." Despite his sarcasm, Belimai seemed to relax.

Harper felt an unwarranted ease. Perhaps he was simply too tired to be afraid anymore. He was glad to be walking through the passing seconds, not chasing them in desperation. This once, he thought, he might have arrived in time.

They walked side by side as the rain poured down over them and the gas lamps flickered in the darkness.

Chapter Four
Fever

*A*s Harper had hoped, he and Belimai boarded the Green-Hill carriage without trouble. As other passengers pushed inside the dark shell of the carriage, Harper was crushed up against Belimai. Steadily both of the seats in the carriage filled. Harper tensed against the weight of the man on his left as the last passenger squeezed into the carriage. Belimai sat silently on Harper's right, pressed between Harper and the carriage wall.

Harper felt each wave of heat and every shudder that wracked Belimai's body. He wished he could see Belimai's face, but the carriage was too dark. When the light from the gas lamps outside flashed through the window, Harper would catch brief glances at Belimai. He saw little more than a stretch of ashen skin and the thin line of Belimai's pale mouth before the carriage plunged forward again into darkness.

Belimai's silence gnawed at Harper. He brushed his hand against Belimai's shoulder. He tried to make more room for Belimai, but he could only move a little before he unintentionally elbowed the man on his left. Belimai slumped against Harper. His skin was burning hot.

"I think I may vomit," Belimai whispered.

The man on Harper's left squirmed back from the two of them.

"You'll be fine," Harper said. "Just try to relax."

"I can't," Belimai groaned. "I really am going to vomit."

"Try to hang on." Harper knew that his words would change nothing, but they were all he could offer.

He wasn't surprised when the man on his left as well as two other travelers evacuated the carriage at the next stop. Waiting in the rain wasn't such a bad thing when compared to riding in a carriage next to a violently ill passenger. To Harper's relief, the rest of the passengers disembarked shortly after the carriage was checked and waved through the city gates. Only he and Belimai were traveling the full distance of the route.

Harper started to move to the other seat to give Belimai more room, but Belimai caught hold of him.

"Stay," Belimai said. "You're warm."

"Are you sure you don't want more space?" Harper asked.

"Not now. Maybe later," Belimai whispered.

He sank down and rested his head on Harper's leg. Belimai's entire body trembled. The skin of his cheek felt fevered even through the thick cotton of Harper's pants.

"I wish it were always this dark," Belimai said. "If only I had just a little..."

"A little what?" Harper asked after Belimai trailed off into silence.

"Ophorium." Belimai jerked upright suddenly. "I'm going to throw up."

He rocked forward and then collapsed down to the carriage floor. Harper reached to catch him, but it was too dark for him to see where Belimai was. Then Harper heard the latch of the carriage door click. Light from the rider's lamps at the front of the carriage poured in. Belimai hung out of the carriage, gripping the door handle for support as he retched.

Harper jumped forward, reaching under Belimai's chest to support his convulsing body as he leaned out of the carriage. Wind and icy pellets of rain slashed in through the open door. Belimai shook and coughed violently, but there was nothing in his stomach to bring up. Harper pulled him back in and slammed the carriage door shut. With a quick practiced flick of his hand, he snapped the lock into place.

"How long has it been since you've had any?"

"Too long, obviously." Belimai's voice was alarmingly soft. He could hardly pull himself back up to the seat cushions. Harper waited in the darkness while Belimai resettled himself, laying his head in Harper's lap again.

Belimai sighed. "Almost three days now."

"Why?" Harper asked.

"I didn't think you'd disapprove—"

"I don't." Harper cut in quickly before Belimai could elude the question. "I just wondered what could get you to do it."

"You don't want to know," Belimai said softly.

"If I didn't want to know, I wouldn't ask." Harper touched Belimai's forehead and then slowly brushed his fingers over the damp kinky mass of his hair. Belimai was silent. Harper knew he couldn't force Belimai to answer.

Perhaps Belimai was even right. Maybe he didn't want to know the answer. If Belimai had at last found another lover who inspired him to change, then it was not news that Harper would relish. What he wanted to hear was his own name.

Harper knew it was contemptible to wish that Belimai's salvation would come through him. It was a deeply selfish need to be a savior, if only for this one man. Still, it was what Harper wanted. He longed for it and at the same time knew that it was not likely to happen.

Only one man meant that much to Belimai; he had ruined himself for Sariel. Harper never forgot that. When he had first read Belimai's legal record, he had been horrified and deeply moved by Belimai's devotion to Sariel. He had read the record over and over, staring at the photograph of Belimai and wishing that he could have saved him.

The silence between them stretched on. Harper stroked Belimai's hair. Belimai's skin radiated a fevered heat, but his breathing was slow and even. Harper wondered if he might be sleeping at last.

Suddenly Belimai jerked as if he had grasped a live electric wire. Choking, inarticulate noises gurgled out of Belimai's throat as the spasms rocked through his chest and stomach. Harper caught Belimai's shuddering body before he crashed to the carriage floor. As suddenly as they had come on, the tremors stopped. Belimai sagged back down against Harper's legs, sweating and limp.

"You weren't supposed to see this," Belimai murmured.

"I'm not seeing much of anything," Harper said. "It's too dark."

"You're not missing anything, trust me." Belimai shifted to his side. "I would have gotten it all over with by the time you came back from your vacation," Belimai said.

"I've seen people in worse shape. It's all right." Harper pushed the sweat-soaked curls back from Belimai's forehead. Belimai's sweat smelled sweetly acrid, like scorched pineapple. It was an unnatural scent, even for a Prodigal.

"I'm so glad to be grouped with the men you've seen in rotten shape. My hope is that someday I will reach the pinnacle of that appalling list. Give me a day or two, and who knows? I think I'm going to vomit again."

Belimai weakly pulled himself upright. He rocked with the motions of the carriage. Harper felt Belimai's body bump against his shoulder. He reached out to steady Belimai, but Belimai shoved his hand away.

"No, it's passed now." Belimai sank back down onto the seat and resettled his head on Harper's leg. "Fucking wretched."

"I can't believe that you were going to go to the Crone in this state." Harper shook his head.

"I didn't know what else to do," Belimai answered. His voice was soft. "I didn't want to get you involved."

"I know." Harper continued stroking Belimai's hair. "But I'm the one who got myself involved. There's nothing you could do about that."

"No, I suppose not. You're really annoying that way, you know."

"Am I?" Harper asked, but Belimai said nothing.

Silence filled the dark emptiness of the carriage. Harper couldn't even hear the rain anymore. They had driven out of the storm. Only the steady rhythm of the horses' hooves beating against the dirt road interrupted the silence of the night. Harper closed his eyes. Sleep seemed very appealing.

"What's it like?" Belimai's voice surprised him. He hadn't thought Belimai was still awake.

"What?" Harper asked.

"Where we're going…" Belimai's voice was slow and groggy.

"What's it like?"

"The Foster Estate? It's big, empty...quite beautiful, really. There are orchards, mostly apple and hazelnut. There's a summer staff there, but that's all. My grandmother stays with my aunt's family at Redcliff. We'll have the place to ourselves."

"Sounds nice. I wish that I wasn't so messed up for my one chance to see the world outside the capital."

"You'll get better. It's not as if I'm going to haul you back to the city after you recover."

"No. Guess not. God, I'm cold." Belimai shuddered.

"You're burning up," Harper whispered.

"Do you think hell will be worse than this?" Belimai murmured, curling his arms in around himself.

"I don't know." Harper closed his eyes again. Belimai's fevered body trembled, and Harper continued stroking his hair. He wished Belimai would fall asleep. It would be easier on both of them.

"Tell me something," Belimai whispered.

"What?" Harper asked.

"Do you ever think about hell?"

"Not if I can help it."

"I used to think about it all the time. I wondered what it was like, now that all the demons had left it."

"A vast, abandoned kingdom of endless silence...if you believe the scriptures," Harper replied easily.

"And do you believe the scriptures, Captain Harper?"

Harper imagined, from Belimai's tone of voice, that Belimai was watching him with that sidelong smirk. It wasn't an odd expression for Belimai; in fact, it suited his features. He often used the expression to mask his own earnestness.

"I imagine we'll discover what's there for ourselves soon enough," Harper said.

"I'll write you about it if I get there before you. I bet it's warm." Belimai's words were garbled under a long yawn. He shivered and then resettled himself.

"Do you want me to cover you with my coat?" Harper asked.

"Harper." Belimai was quiet for a long moment. "You can't keep giving your own things up for other people. You need to be a little selfish sometimes."

"It's no trouble. I'm not cold."

"We're both cold..." Belimai drifted into silence. He lay limp against Harper and, at last, fell asleep.

Harper had known he would. Only in the few minutes before he passed out did Belimai completely lose his tones of sarcasm and cynicism. Some nights, if Harper kept him talking, Belimai could almost sound sweet.

Harper relaxed back against the cushions of the seat. He closed his eyes and slept.

Steadily the night gave way to morning, and bright light poured in through the carriage window. Belimai rolled over so that his face pressed into the shadows of the seat cushions. Harper woke and gazed out at the passing rows of apple trees. The air was sweet with the perfume of wildflowers and fallen rain. He was nearly home.

Chapter Five
Angel

The estate house was as Harper remembered. The dark building rose above the outer walls and towered over the oak trees lining the drive. The huge walls were first erected when the estate served as a church garrison. They stood, as they had for generations, awaiting a last assault of ancient heretics. From the narrow windows high in the walls to the vast stables, the estate remained in a warring past. Instead of gas lamps, iron torch-holders hung over the massive stone entry.

Though the grounds and building were immaculate and clearly kept up, the quiet made the estate house seem abandoned. It felt deeply isolated. Not just separated from the rest of civilization by distance, but lost in another age.

Each time Harper returned, he recalled thinking that the torch-holders should be refitted for new gas fixtures. But then he always forgot and ended up leaving them until the next time he came. He wondered if his father had perhaps done the same thing. Perhaps generations of his ancestors had done so, and slowly the estate house had been left further and further in the past, until it at last became this towering relic.

Harper rapped at the carved double doors. The sound wasn't much, but it carried through the stillness. A moment later a slot in one of the doors opened and a young man, dressed in the estate colors of blue and white, grinned out at Harper.

His name was Giles and he was the eldest son of Mrs. Kately, the housekeeper. Harper's annual visits always afforded him a glimpse of the progress of Giles' maturity. This year Giles sported a wispy brown mustache that looked like something he might have bought in a costume shop rather than grown. The way he stroked his chin told Harper that he was rather proud of the thing. Giles pulled aside the heavy bolt and heaved at the door.

"Good morning, Master William. It's a pleasure to see you back at the estate, sir." Giles inclined his head and then noticed Belimai.

In the bright morning sun, it was obvious that Belimai's clothes were mismatched and the wrong sizes. His skin looked waxy and his hair was a wild, black mass. He clenched his eyes closed against the light.

Giles stared at him.

"Good morning to you also, sir," Giles said after a moment.

Belimai groaned slightly in response.

"Giles." Harper called the young man's attention away from Belimai. "Will you inform Mrs. Kately that I have a guest with me and that he is ill? We'll be taking meals upstairs."

"Yes, sir." Giles bowed and then quietly left the entry hall.

"Are you all right?" Harper asked once they were alone.

Belimai slowly cracked his eyes open wide enough to study his surroundings.

"Too damn bright," Belimai said quietly.

The marble floor gleamed, reflecting the shafts of sunlight that poured in through the windows. Though tapestries of martyred saints no longer hung from the walls, the estate house still held remnants of its early history. Gilded crosses were etched into the face of each door and over every archway. Narrow, stained glass windows infused the morning light with vivid colors. Tiny, luminous visions of angels in battle and sinners in torment shone from high up in the walls.

Harper followed Belimai's gaze up to a furious, red-eyed angel of vengeance. The image was one of a hundred that Harper had seen day-in and out during his youth and then again during his studies at St. Bennet's. Like the images of the cross, angels had become so familiar to Harper that he hardly noticed them at all anymore.

Belimai's pupils dilated and contracted. His lips moved fractionally, but no sound came out. Harper wondered if he was hallucinating.

"Belimai," Harper said. "It's just a stained glass window."

"She looks like your sister," Belimai said at last.

Harper looked back up at the window. Belimai was right. It did look like Joan. Not the sweet, brown-eyed girl of his memories, but the furious woman she had become after Peter Roffcale's murder. The angel hung over him like an accusation.

"Harper," Belimai whispered.

"What?" Harper glanced back to Belimai.

His face had gone a bloodless white. He swayed, and Harper placed an arm on his shoulder to steady him.

"It's all right," Belimai whispered. "I'm just..." Belimai crumpled. Harper caught him and lifted him up into his arms.

The closest bedroom was the nursery. Harper doubted that Belimai would appreciate the décor, but at the moment he wasn't likely to notice it. The walls were painted in bright childish colors and Harper's name was embroidered across the trim of the coverlet on the bed.

As Harper lay Belimai down on the bed, he realized that Belimai had regained consciousness. He stared at the far wall.

"My God," Belimai muttered, "are there clouds all over the walls?"

"Yes. You should get out of these clothes." When Harper reached for Belimai's coat, Belimai flinched back from him. Then he suddenly cupped his hands over his face.

"Are you going to be sick?" Harper felt a slight burst of panic as he glanced around for a basin of some kind.

"No." Belimai slowly lowered his arms. "For a moment I thought I was in the Inquisition House again." Belimai scowled at the far wall, with its scattering of fluffy white clouds.

"Where the hell am I?" Belimai demanded.

"We're in the nursery. And you need to get undressed and lay down." Harper gently tugged off Belimai's shoes and then took his coat. "These are the only rooms that have been improved much in the last hundred years. Hopefully the pumped water and heating will make up for the blue sky and little clouds painted all over the walls and ceiling."

"Maggots," Belimai mumbled.

"Maggots?" Harper asked.

"There are sticky piles of maggots eating through the walls."

"They're not real," Harper said.

"I know." Belimai continued staring. "It's quite a convincing hallucination though."

Belimai seemed oddly calm. Harper wondered if it was because he was too tired to react or if Belimai was already deeply familiar with hallucinations. Harper watched him for a moment. Belimai continued to glare at the wall as if it were to blame for what he saw.

"You know what the worst thing about them is?" Belimai didn't look at Harper when he spoke.

"What?"

"The fact that they're coming from my own mind." Belimai forced an unnaturally bright smile. "All those ugly little bodies are worming out of ugly little me." He continued staring forward at the wall. Harper began to worry.

"I never realized I was so familiar with maggots," Belimai continued. "So white and pulpy. Their wet little mouths never stop chewing. They glisten."

"Try not to think about them. You're going to have to try to sleep." Harper gently took hold of Belimai's arm and worked his shirt off him. It was damp with sweat. Harper tossed it aside. The skin of Belimai's chest was deathly pale, and the scars left by the prayer engines looked alarmingly red.

"I don't want to close my eyes," Belimai said. "I don't want to keep seeing them inside my head."

"They'll go away, I promise." Harper stripped off the rest of Belimai's clothes. Belimai took a short, sharp breath each time Harper's hands contacted his skin. His yellow eyes searched the far wall. Harper pushed him back down into the blankets.

"You have to sleep, Belimai," he said.

"No. I don't," Belimai whispered, but he wasn't even looking at Harper. His eyes were wide and focused on the empty space to Harper's left.

Belimai's eyes had been open so long that tears welled up and dribbled down the sides of his face.

"Belimai," Harper said softly. "Close your eyes."

"Close yours," Belimai hissed.

"Why?" Harper asked.

"I don't want you to see me like this." Belimai pulled his gaze away from the ceiling and stared hard at Harper. "Close your eyes."

Harper closed his eyes.

He heard Belimai shifting through the blankets.

Harper cracked his eyes just enough to take in a shadowed impression of Belimai's motions. Belimai crouched on the far side of the bed. He was still for a moment, then he hunched over and vomited into a bedside washbasin. Harper closed his eyes again and gave Belimai his privacy. After a few minutes, the room seemed too quiet. Harper opened his eyes. Belimai knelt on the floor. Harper watched Belimai cram himself under the small bed and collapse.

As Harper lifted Belimai back up onto the bed, he noticed with alarm that blots of blood colored Belimai's chest. The holy words scarring Belimai's body were bleeding. As Harper watched, a delicate line on Belimai's shoulder split and bright red beads of blood welled up. Letter after letter opened, as if a phantom blade were re-tracing each of the ophorium-packed scars that the prayer engines had laid down.

Harper reached down to daub the blood away with his hand-kerchief. Belimai's eyes snapped open.

"No!" Belimai shouted.

Before Harper could react, Belimai punched him hard in the chest. Harper grabbed Belimai's hand and caught the other as Belimai took a swipe at his face. Instinctively Harper reached for his handcuffs. He quickly locked Belimai's hands to the headboard. It was easy to do, but Harper hated it. It felt like betrayal to restrain Belimai just as the Inquisition had trained him to do.

Belimai fought hard against the handcuffs, screaming and kicking. He twisted and jerked until his wrists bled. Then, in absolute exhaustion, he collapsed back to the bed.

Harper backed away and sat down on the floor. He stared up at the orange sun painted on the ceiling. When he had been a child, it had seemed magically real. The entire world had been as simplistic as that painting. Bright blue days and deep, sleepy nights had encircled his existence while his parents enfolded him in a constant sense of adoration. Harper wished he could still feel so perfectly happy.

He didn't know when exactly he had lost his hold on that life. Small, corrosive deceptions had steadily eaten away at his innocence. He had learned that his father was actually a stepfather and that Joan was only a stepsister. He'd often lied about that, sometimes even to himself. He had answered to two different names: Foster, at chapel, and Harper, at home. He wore gloves, as his sister and stepfather did, to disguise a Prodigal nature that he did not possess. He still wore them now. Sometimes, when he had been young, he would stare down at his gloved hands and forget that he was not one of them.

He had told lie upon lie about his family, about his beliefs and even himself. After years of it, all he could remember were the lies.

When his stepfather had asked him why he was becoming an Inquisitor, Harper hadn't dared to give him an honest answer. Harper had flushed with shame, knowing that what drove him was loneliness. He had burned with the desire to be with Prodigals. He had ached to caress their bodies, to kiss their hot mouths. But only an Inquisitor could consort with the sons of devils and not be suspected of heresy. He had wanted to find a Prodigal lover but not be hanged for it. He hadn't even known how to say those things. His longing had been shadowed beneath his fear and shame.

At last he had blurted out a string of lies, claiming a desire to avenge his real father. He had ranted over his family heritage, eight generations of service to the Cross. He had sneered at his stepfather and railed against the Prodigals in Hells Below. His words had tumbled out in a red-faced rush of confused passion. At some point he had crossed the line of forgiveness. Harper could still remember the pain in his stepfather's face.

Harper looked down at his bare hands. Clean, white priest's hands. They didn't seem like they should be his at all.

"Master William?" A soft female voice intruded into Harper's thoughts. Mrs. Kately smiled at him from the doorway. She was a plain woman, but her warm smiles lent her beauty.

"Giles said you brought a friend." She stepped into the room. "I was wondering which rooms you wanted aired—" She stopped the moment she caught sight of Belimai.

"He's very sick," Harper said. "Delirious."

Mrs. Kately closed the door behind her and then walked closer to where Belimai lay unconscious and shackled to the headboard. She frowned, but in that slight, controlled manner that was common among household servants.

"Should I send for a physician?" Mrs. Kately asked at last.

"No. He should recover on his own if we just let him rest and keep him fed."

"I see." Mrs. Kately continued to gaze at Belimai. Her placid, professional expression smoothed over any private feelings she might have had. Harper watched her, knowing that Belimai's freedom depended on her complicity.

He was always surprised at how much younger she was than he expected her to be. She had been pregnant and twice Harper's age when she first came to work at the estate house. At the time, she had struck Harper as a very old woman. She had been an adult and he, a child. The divide between the two had seemed infinite. Now the difference of ten years seemed like nothing.

Mrs. Kately looked at the ruined heap of clothes Harper had tossed aside.

"He's going to need something to wear," Mrs. Kately said.

"Yes," Harper agreed.

"He resembles the previous Mr. Harper, doesn't he?" she said suddenly.

"Yes." Harper knew there was no way of hiding Belimai's Prodigal blood from her, not at this point. Many people who had lived all their lives in the country had no idea of what a Prodigal looked like, but Mrs. Kately had lived in the capital when she was a girl. She had only moved out to the countryside once she discovered that she was with child and without husband.

Harper's stepfather had hired her and insisted that she be addressed as "Mrs.," just as any decent woman would have been. In return Mrs. Kately had kept silent about Harper's stepfather and Joan. Harper hoped that she would be willing to keep Belimai's secret as well.

Mrs. Kately nodded slowly to herself and then looked back at Harper.

"He should probably stay here in the nursery until he's better. The other rooms can be drafty. I'll have the cook make soup for him. Hopefully he'll be able to keep that down." Again that minute, a frown twitched at the corners of her mouth. "We're going to have to look after him ourselves until he can be counted on not to give himself away."

"I'll take care of him," Harper told her.

"You'll need to sleep sometime." Mrs. Kately said it simply, not as if she were arguing with him, but rather commenting on the matter to herself. "I'll see if I can find some clothes for him, and you're going to need something to sit on other than the floor." She looked pointedly at where Harper sat on the floor.

Harper stood, suddenly realizing how foolish he must have looked. He hadn't hunched despondently on the floor since he had been a child. Standing, he was much taller than Mrs. Kately. She had to crane her head back a little to meet his gaze.

"I'll bring something up to eat as soon as the cook has it ready." Mrs. Kately started for the door.

"Thank you, for everything," Harper said.

Mrs. Kately looked back and suddenly gave him a full smile.

"It's good to have you back home, Master William," she said.

"It's good to be back," Harper replied, and for the first time in years, he realized that he wasn't lying.

Chapter Six
Handcuffs

*B*elimai slept often, and he dreamed of horrible things. Harper watched as, time after time, Belimai jerked awake, choking on a scream. On the fifth day Belimai's cries burst into a demonic roar. His voice tore through the air, exploding outward like thunder. Two windows shattered, and Harper dropped to the floor to avoid the rending force.

When Harper stood again, Belimai lay on his side, his arms still stretched out and cuffed to the headboard. He opened his eyes and slowly tried to pull his arms down to his sides. He frowned at the handcuffs and then glanced at Harper.

"What did you do to my hands?" Belimai asked as he again tried to bring his arms down.

"Handcuffs," Harper said.

"I had no idea you were in the mood for romance." Belimai's voice was weak but far calmer than it had been in days.

Belimai looked around the room as if he had just arrived there. He frowned at the clusters of white clouds, which burst out like rashes across the blue walls. The big gold sun painted over the ceiling received the same disturbed scowl.

"You're in the nursery," Harper explained as Belimai squinted at a huge red toy chest across the room.

"Were you trying to share the horror of your childhood?" Belimai asked.

Harper was pleased to hear cynicism ring through Belimai's voice. For days Belimai had only hissed garbled curses and strings of disconnected words. His voice had been an animal's, able to convey nothing more than his pain. Now for the first time, Belimai's intellect seemed to have returned.

"The nursery's farthest from the servant's quarters, and it's the best-insulated part of the house. I thought it would be wisest if we kept things as quiet as possible," Harper said.

Belimai nodded slowly and then sniffed at the air. He frowned.

"Something stinks." He sniffed again and then glanced down at his own blood-caked body and the stained sheets that hung across him. "It's me, isn't it?"

"Give me a few minutes. I'll get some clean bedding and a basin of warm water." Harper stepped back from the bedside.

"And my hands?" Belimai rattled the handcuffs.

"I'll get the keys." Harper had the keys in his pocket, but he wasn't sure how long Belimai's coherence would last. "It may take me a little while to get everything. Just rest and relax."

Belimai nodded, though Harper noticed that he continued to shift his hands against the cuffs. He pulled and squeezed his palms back and forth, attempting to work his way out of them. Harper gathered clean linens as well as a basin of warm water and a sponge.

When he returned, he found Belimai passed out again with one arm free and dangling off the bed. Harper pulled a chair up to the bedside and began sponging Belimai clean. Belimai opened his eyes blearily.

"I keep dreaming that I'm back in the Inquisition House. They want Sariel's name. I hate being in that place."

Harper sponged the sweat from Belimai's face and then washed his throat and shoulders.

"If you feel up to it tomorrow, I'll show you around the grounds. Try dreaming about that instead."

"Thank you, Harper." Belimai was almost unconscious when the words slipped out. "I don't usually thank you, but I should."

"You're welcome," Harper replied. Belimai fell back asleep. Harper rolled Belimai over a few inches and pulled the soiled sheets from under his body.

Years ago when he had been at college, Edward had shown him how to change sheets from under a sleeping man. Harper had spent a few weeks after that stealing the sheets from under his fellow seminary students. He had gotten rather good at it. He had even managed to steal the linens from under a visiting abbot once.

Harper shoved the bloodied bedding out into the hall. Mrs. Kately could decide if they were worth washing or if she just wanted to burn them. Harper dropped back down in the chair at Belimai's bedside. Absently he wondered how he would replace the shattered windows. They could wait until later; for the moment he enjoyed the light breeze that drifted into the room. It was the first time in well over a week that Harper hadn't been preoccupied with some immediate emergency.

He wondered what he and Belimai would do tomorrow. An excitement began to build in him. They were free to do what ever they pleased. These lands were his, and Belimai was finally well enough to enjoy them with him. He wondered what part of the estate Belimai would like best.

Harper smiled to himself. Perhaps this time he would stay long enough to actually have those torch-holders refitted.

"Daydreaming?" A woman's voice suddenly broke through his thoughts.

Harper leapt to his feet and spun to see his sister sitting just inside the frame of the open window. Her cropped hair drooped in dirty strands around her face. Dust coated her jacket and pants. She smiled with hesitant slowness, as if she were cautiously trespassing on ground that used to be hers.

Harper also smiled, but he didn't rush forward and sweep her up in a hug as he once would have. She seemed out of place indoors, like some mythic child raised by beasts in the wilderness. The black nails that she used to spend hours clipping and bleaching now jutted from her finger tips like talons. Her red eyes roamed restlessly from Harper's face to his hands, and then to the gun holster hanging below his left arm.

"It's been a while," Harper said. "How have you been?"

"Can't complain. You?"

"Busy." Harper frowned at the awkwardness of their exchange. They sounded like distant acquaintances at a wake. "Have you been getting enough food? You look thinner."

"I've been just fine, Will. Mica's been teaching me to tell fortunes. I've been making a good living. The people at Good Commons have been watching out for me."

"That's good," Harper replied. "Have you seen Edward?"

" I...I've kept track of him, but we haven't spoken..." She glanced up at the bright blue sky on the ceiling and shook her head. "How could we? What could I possibly say that would make things all right between us?"

"You could let him know that you aren't dead."

"Do you honestly think it would do him any good? At least this way there's a clean ending. He can remember me as a faithful, darling wife who died at the hands of criminals. It's sad, but God knows it has to be better than telling him that I was in love with another man. Or that I'm a Prodigal. Or that I went out of my mind and burned his house down. What would it do to him to know those things?"

"I don't know, but I think he deserves the truth."

"You wouldn't tell him, would you?" She stared at him, and Harper shook his head.

"You know I wouldn't tell anyone." The thought made him glance back to where Belimai lay sleeping. Joan's secrets had given him a reason to approach Belimai.

"Who's your guest?" Joan cocked her head to the side and looked past Harper to the bed.

"Belimai Sykes. He's recovering from a bout of flu." Harper gave her the same lie he and Mrs. Kately had offered the staff.

"I've seen him before...at St. Christopher's. He helped me."

"He was also at Scott-Beck's office when you torched it. You nearly killed him." Harper tried to keep the recrimination out of his voice, but it was hard. Not only had Joan nearly killed Belimai, but she had destroyed any evidence that Harper might have used to bring charges against Abbot Greeley for his involvement.

"I don't remember much about that." She ran her hand through her hair and a thin cloud of dust drifted up from her fingers into the bright morning light. "Do you have him handcuffed for a reason?"

Harper simply ignored the question. He had kept Joan's secrets from Belimai; the least he could do was give Belimai the same courtesy.

"Why did you come to see me?" Harper asked.

"You aren't going to hurt him, are you?" Joan asked.

"The last thing in this world that I would do is hurt him," Harper said flatly. "Now, tell me why you're here."

"It's Nick Sariel—"

"Doesn't anything happen without involving that man?" The name alone was becoming a physical pain to Harper. Joan stepped back from him slightly.

"I didn't think the two of you were on such bad terms."

"He blames me for Peter's death, and I—" Harper cut himself off. Even when he and Joan had been at their closest, Harper had kept his desires and temptations to himself. "I'm just sick of every living Prodigal thinking I'm his enemy."

"I know you're not my enemy, Will."

Harper was surprised at the sudden softness in his sister's tone. She smiled at him.

"Things have just been so confused...so hard. I haven't always been thinking straight, but I've never hated you. I've never blamed you."

"I know." Harper took the four steps that closed the distance between them. "You know that I don't blame you either, don't you? I'm sorry as hell about Peter and for Edward, but mostly I just miss having you around."

Harper took her hands carefully in his and gave her a reassuring squeeze, just as he had always done in the past. The same small gesture had always conveyed his love: after their mother's death, after their father's disappearance, throughout their lives. He hadn't known that one gesture was all his sister had been waiting for, just a single sign that they were still brother and sister.

"I've missed you too, Will." Joan pressed against his chest, hugging him. "It's been like some terrible nightmare that I can't wake up from. All I could think of was how furious I was, how much I missed Peter. And I kept thinking that I should have been there with him. I should have been down in Hells Below living with him, not hiding behind Edward and you, pretending I was someone I'm not."

"Even if you had been there, you couldn't have saved him." Harper wrapped his arms around her.

"I might have," she whispered against his shirt. "If I had been with him instead of running and hiding, who knows how it would have turned out?" Harper heard the tremble in her voice and the slight pause as she pulled herself back from the point of tears. She sniffed and drew a step back from him.

"This time I want to do things differently, but I need your help."

"They've arrested Sariel, haven't they?" In the back of his mind, Harper had known they would. Sariel was one of the few remaining Prodigals who could fly. Between that and his involvement in Good Commons, he made the perfect scapegoat for the murder of Lord Cedric's niece.

"They took him in for questioning six days ago, and we've heard nothing from him since."

"They're probably torturing a confession out of him."

"But he hasn't done anything," Joan said.

"He doesn't have to have done anything. There are plenty of crimes that have already been committed. They'll just assign one of those to him."

"Can you get him out?" Joan asked.

"Possibly." Harper felt suddenly very tired. Part of him didn't even want to get Sariel out. A deep, bitter vein of malice within him wanted Sariel to suffer as Belimai had suffered.

He wondered what Belimai would do if he found out that Sariel was in Inquisition custody. Would he collapse back into addiction? Or more likely, and far worse, he would confess to the murder himself to get Sariel released.

"It's not just Nick, either," Joan went on. "Two days ago they took Edward into custody also."

For a moment, Harper was simply too stunned by the idea to react.

"They took him in for questioning. I think they suspect that I'm the one who killed Scott-Beck," Joan said.

"I doubt it has to do with that." Harper's head was beginning to throb with tense pain. Somewhere in the very back of his thoughts, a count was beginning. He was already two days too late to save Edward. Every passing moment brought Edward closer to breaking down into a forced confession.

"Why else would they take Edward in?" Joan asked. "He's never done anything wrong in his life."

"It's not your fault, Joan. If anything, it's mine." Harper pressed his fingers up against the sides of his temple as if he could somehow just push the sharp bursts of pain back from his awareness. "I'll have to leave right away."

"We can go right now if you want. I'll need a fresh horse, but there should be several in the stable—"

"No. I need you to stay here." Harper dug into his pocket and handed the keys to his handcuffs to his sister. "Look after Belimai for me. He's going to need someone to be here with him. Just, whatever you do, don't tell him about Sariel, all right?"

"I haven't even agreed to stay," Joan protested.

"Joan, please don't make me waste time arguing with you about this. Edward is in a House of the Inquisition. If I get to him quickly, I might be able to do something, but I can't just leave Belimai here alone."

"Fine. I'll stay."

"Thank you." Harper hugged her once quickly. He turned to go and then stopped for a moment to watch Belimai shift in his sleep.

"Tell him I'm sorry," Harper said to his sister, and then he left.

Chapter Seven
Rust

*H*arper drew in a last drag from his cigarette, then flicked the short butt into a murky stream of rainwater trickling past his feet. The ember extinguished with a hiss that was almost inaudible beneath the wail of the city alarm. Searchlights flared through the dark sky, illuminating the ornate faces of the nearby buildings. The lights swept over the carved facade of the High Cross Library and then shot through the crystal dome of the Water Works Building. All along the Civic Plaza, Inquisitors rushed from building to building, evacuating workmen, academics, and public servants. Teams of acolytes raced back and forth, shutting off the gas lines.

Harper watched as the last engineers were hustled out of the Water Works Building. He ducked back into the alley beside the Notary Building as an elderly Sister of Scriptures was dragged shrieking from the library. Two angry Inquisitors carried her away.

Just ahead of him, the glass housing of a streetlamp exploded. Flames burst up through the pipes. Blinding blue light arced into the air as the lime filament seared to vapor. Harper pulled his cap low over his eyes and rushed out from the narrow alley. He strode purposefully past two white-faced acolytes who gaped at the geyser of flame.

"Don't just stand there with your gobs open! Get clear before the gas main blows!" Harper shouted over the howling siren. The acolytes immediately fled back behind the fire-barricades. Harper strode ahead into the Water Works Building.

"This is the last warning!" Harper shouted as he walked across the marble foyer toward the pump rooms. Shafts of light splintered and flashed around him as another searchlight swept across the crystal dome above. Shadows twisted and jumped, then the search-light passed and darkness enveloped the room. No one seemed to have lingered. Harper continued to call out as he walked to the maintenance stairs, just in case.

"We need everyone out of this building. There's been a rupture in the street gas line. This is the last warning." As Harper descended the winding iron staircase, the noise from the plaza faded. A deep thrum pulsed out from the turbines. It vibrated through the massive pipelines and through the rungs of the stairs spiraling down around them.

With all the gas lines shut down, the only sources of illumination remaining were dim phosphor lamps that hung from the handrail. They bathed Harper in a dull green glow. He unclipped one of the cylindrical lamps and continued down. As he descended, the air grew thick and stagnant.

At the bottom of the staircase, Harper entered a long concrete corridor. Heavy iron hatches, each leading to a maintenance shaft, lined the walls. Harper checked the letters and numbers engraved above each of the hatches. *Mt 22-21, Mrk 1-14, Mt 10-8.*

"Matthew, Mark, and Matthew again," he whispered.

One of his first assignments in the Inquisition had been in these maintenance shafts. Harper had spent nearly a week searching for a lost Prodigal child. Eventually he had found her, but in the intervening time he'd learned how completely the maintenance shafts infiltrated the city. Anywhere a major water pipe existed, a maintenance shaft ran alongside it. And there were water pipes everywhere. The only problem was finding the right one.

Harper held up the phosphor lamp and read the encoding over the hatch he had just reached, *Deut 15-6.* "Deuteronomy, chapter 15, verse 6. 'Lend unto many nations, but borrow of none, so shall thou reign over many.' Pipes for the Banker's rows, I'll bet."

He turned and walked past three more hatches. At last, he found the one marked *Deut 19-18.* Harper smirked at the wordplay of the chosen verse: *And the judges shall make diligent inquisition.*

The hatch screeched a sharp protest as Harper forced the rusted bearings of the hinge to swing open. Rank yellow water dribbled out from the open shaft. The air smelled both stale and putrid. Clearly, the water pipes leading to the Brighton Inquisition House hadn't been checked in a few years. Harper ducked inside, pulling the hatch closed behind him.

The shaft was narrow and tall. Water seeped from the pipe running overhead and spattered down onto Harper's cap. A stagnant stream of water rippled around his ankles. Harper moved fast through the dank pools, his phosphor lamp casting an eerie green glow over the water. Where the maintenance shaft split into a Y juncture, he scanned the concrete walls for the few short letters that indicated the streets far above him.

Movement soothed his mind. It almost drowned out the incessant count of seconds that ran through his head. He had, perhaps, another half hour before the Inquisitors completely evacuated the Civic Plaza. After that, it would only take a quarter of an hour before one of them discovered that the gas lines were fine. Harper had simply tampered with the intake valves of a few streetlamps to ensure that their explosive displays set off the city alarms.

Harper broke into a run. It eased him to finally take action. Forced to watch and wait for Belimai to surface from his private torture all of the previous week, he had felt helpless. It had drawn him perilously close to prayer, and Harper knew he no longer had the faith for that.

But motion fed him. His muscles devoured the space between himself and his desire. He poured himself into the pure sensation of his body. He leapt up onto an access ladder and climbed into an adjoining shaft. He raced through the second shaft, ducking and jumping the smaller water pipes that cut across his path.

At last he stood directly under the Brighton Inquisition House. He clipped the phosphor lamp onto a narrow pipe and gripped the rusted entry hatch with both hands. Even through his gloves, the metal felt rough. Harper shoved hard against the hatch, feeling the ragged metal bite into the palm of his right hand. The thick seal of rust cracked with a low scrape, and the hatch swung open. Harper crawled forward through the series of tiny chambers that buffered the Inquisition House in case of a burst pipe. He climbed a narrow rung ladder up to a final hatch, forced it open, and pulled himself out onto a cracked tile floor.

The pump room was cluttered with an assortment of mops, brooms, and valve wrenches. Harper wrung the water out of his pant cuffs. His right palm stung. He squeezed his hand closed around the cut. He straightened his cap and left the pump room.

The Inquisition House wasn't empty, but there were fewer men than usual. Most were still out at the Civic Plaza, Harper guessed. He climbed an immaculate white staircase to the third floor. His heart beat in his chest like a jackrabbit in a wire trap. An acolyte passed him. They exchanged brief smiles.

Harper strolled past two more Inquisitors and let himself into the records room with his own key. Once he had pulled the door closed, he raced to the open cases. He flipped rapidly through break-ins, stabbings, robberies, and heresies.

At last he found Edward's name. He was being held as a witness for prosecution against Nick Sariel and another undisclosed suspect. Harper folded the page of charges up, slipped it into his pocket, and then looked over the record of Edward's testimony. Harper knew better than to feel betrayed at seeing his own name disclosed. He hadn't expected Edward to be able to hold out against trained Confessors.

Harper added the testimony to his pocket and then scanned through the files for Nick Sariel's name among Captain Brandson's cases. The file was nearly an inch thick. Harper skipped over Nick Sariel's past crimes and dug out the recent accusations. An unsigned confession waited in the file. Harper found his own initials penciled in several times beside the word *accomplice*. The handwriting wasn't Brandson's; it was Abbot Greeley's.

For a moment Harper simply stared at the page. He didn't know why it surprised him that Abbot Greeley would frame him for murder. Greeley hated him, and Harper was a liability to him. And yet Harper hadn't expected the abbot to sink so far.

Harper pocketed the confession and then dropped Nick Sariel's entire file inside another sheaf of papers containing cases that were up for dismissal. It was doubtful that Nick would be released, but at least the lost paperwork would delay his interrogation.

From the floors below, Harper heard a rising rumble of voices. The first of the Inquisitors were returning from the false alarm at the Civic Plaza. Soon, men would come bustling in to file their reports. Harper thought he heard familiar voices coming up the stairs.

He slipped out of the records room and took the back stairs down to the first floor. He passed a few other Inquisitors, but they took as little note of him as they did of each other. The broad black lines of his uniform melted into the mass of other Inquisitors on the first floor.

Harper's pulse beat wildly. If he was caught now, he could offer no reasonable explanation. The idea of fighting his way free was ludicrous. Inquisitors were everywhere. The brilliant white halls were filled with the whispers of their black coats. Men bumped and jostled past Harper. For the first time in his life, Harper felt unsafe among them.

From a distance he caught sight of Miller. As usual, Reynolds was beside him. Harper dropped back, pacing himself alongside an acolyte. He kept his gaze averted as Miller and Reynolds passed him.

Just ahead, Harper noted a shock of red hair amidst the sea of black caps. Captain Brandson had forgotten his cap again. Harper whispered silent thanks for that. Miller and Reynolds might not have been watching for him, but Brandson would be.

Harper quickly turned down the hall and took a back corridor to the witness holding cells. He couldn't get past the heavy security in the Prodigal section, but at least he could try to free Edward.

Harper didn't know the young man standing guard, and he hoped that the man didn't recognize him either. Harper stopped himself from pulling his cap a little lower.

"I need to take one of the witnesses down to the engines." Harper paused as if the name weren't burning on his lips. "Talbott. I believe the first name is Edward."

The young guard hardly looked beyond the shining silver insignias on Harper's collar. He scanned through the ledger of the prisoners and then pushed the book and a cell key to Harper. Harper paused only an instant as he glanced at the previous signatures in the prisoner ledger. He signed in Brandson's initials, took the key, and went to Edward's cell.

Two cells down another Inquisitor was checking in on a witness of his own. Harper hoped that Edward was still cognizant enough to keep quiet. He unlocked the door and stepped into the small cell.

Edward crouched on a narrow cot with his legs drawn up and his face pressed down into his knees. The confessor had not been gentle with him. His right arm was bandaged from the elbow down. Splints jutted out from under his first two fingers. Edward didn't even glance up.

"Don't take me back there," Edward whispered. "I'll sign whatever you want. Just don't take me back."

Harper closed the cell door and strode to Edward. He clamped his hand over Edward's mouth and tilted his head back. Edward looked up into Harper's face. His eyes went wide and he gave a muffled gasp against Harper's gloved palm.

"I can get you out of here," Harper whispered, "but afterward you're going to be a wanted man."

Edward nodded. Harper drew his hand back. He was shocked when Edward lunged forward and gripped him in a hard, desperate embrace.

"Will, thank God you came! Thank God," Edward whispered against Harper's neck.

It felt good to have Edward so close against his body, but for all the wrong reasons. Harper returned the hug briefly, then pulled back. "We're not out of here yet. You have to keep calm, all right?"

"Yes, of course." Edward swallowed a deep breath of air and nodded.

"Are you hurt anywhere aside from your arm?"

"Some bruises, that's all."

"Good." Harper unclipped his silver handcuffs and closed one of the cuffs around Edward's uninjured left hand. He locked the other around his own right wrist, but so loosely that he could easily slip his hand free.

"One last thing. The old woman I left with you, do you know where they took her?" Harper asked.

"They didn't take her anywhere." Edward closed his eyes for a moment. "They killed her."

"Of course. She was the only witness." A chill rushed through Harper as he realized how effortlessly Abbot Greeley disposed of the people who opposed him.

"We have to go." Harper opened the door and walked Edward out into the hall. He had been worried that Edward might give them away, but Edward kept his head down and walked with the slow dread of a prisoner on his way to the prayer engines.

Harper handed the cell key to the guard and took the prisoner ledger. As he glanced over the ledger, he noticed that Captain Brandson's initials appeared only a column below where Harper had signed them. Brandson hadn't noticed that he had already been signed in. The same initials twice weren't that noticeable, but a third time would be apparent, even to the careless young guard. Harper copied another three initials from higher in the ledger and then slid the book back to the guard.

Without waiting for the young man to respond, Harper pulled Edward forward and headed down the main hall of the Inquisition House. He had to fight his own urge to move fast. It was the sheerest luck that Brandson hadn't noticed the forged initials when he signed the ledger. Harper had no doubt that Brandson would notice them when he left the cells.

Once they reached the back stairs, Harper slipped the handcuffs off and urged Edward ahead.

"No matter what happens, keep going until you reach the pump room. There'll be a maintenance hatch open there. The shafts are coded to the streets overhead, so you'll know where you're going," Harper told him as they went.

"But—"

"Just in case," Harper whispered. Far down the hall, he heard the distinct sound of Brandson's voice rising over the quiet. It would only be a moment before Brandson raised the alarm. Then the entire Inquisition House would be locked down and searched.

"Run," Harper told Edward.

They took the stairs fast and then tore across the distance of basement to reach the pump room. Just as Harper pulled the pump room door shut, the alarm began wailing through the halls. Harper helped Edward into the maintenance shaft.

"It's pitch black in here," Edward whispered.

"Keep climbing down through the next two hatches. I left a lamp there." Harper pulled the hatch above him shut and twisted it closed as tightly as he could. So long as no one thought to connect this escape with the maintenance shafts, he and Edward had a chance of escaping. Harper was betting that Brandson would search the building and surrounding streets first, assuming that the only escape could be above ground.

Despite his lack of faith, Harper prayed he was right.

Chapter Eight
Steam

*H*arper led Edward through shaft after shaft. For the first hour, they traveled in silence. The only noise came from the packs of water rats that scampered over the water pipes and scattered as Harper and Edward approached.

At last Edward whispered a few questions to Harper. He wanted to know where they were and how Harper knew. He asked why Harper had brought the old woman to him and why she had been killed. Harper gave him short, quick answers. It was the way they had always conversed.

Even in college, when he had been deep in his anatomical studies, Edward had been an extrovert. Silence was foreign to his nature. In the past, Edward's constant flow of conversation had annoyed Harper. Now Harper felt relieved to hear Edward's voice. The sound reassured Harper that he had not come too late. The Confessors had hurt Edward, but not destroyed him.

"I think Raddly might put us up for the night," Edward whispered as they crawled through a low shaft.

"Raddly...Didn't he vomit in a deacon's memorial urn?"

"Yes. But I think the port was to blame for that. He's a nice fellow."

Harper tilted the phosphor lamp back so that he could read the letters above an intersecting tunnel.

"We're directly under Bluerow Street," he whispered back to Edward.

"Lottie Hampston lived on Bluerow, didn't she?" Edward asked.

"I don't recall." Harper swung down into the larger shaft and then helped Edward through. The once-white bandages on Edward's arm were now soiled with grease and mold. Spots of blood seeped through.

"What about Waterstone?" Edward asked.

"Who?" Harper glanced back.

"Richard Waterstone. Don't you remember? He could go on about poetry for years."

"Was he covered with moles?" Harper had a clear memory of catching a young man named Richard in the showers. He had had a beautiful back with a line of three moles just above his ass.

"Beauty marks," Edward replied. "Yes, that was him. Why don't we go look him up?"

"I don't recall enough about him to think of why we would look him up, so I doubt I can speak to why we shouldn't," Harper replied.

They reached another hatch, and Harper crouched down to work it open. His arms were aching. Edward hunched down beside him.

"Waterstone's father is the owner of the *Daily Word*. Richard's got a position as chief editor. We could go to him with the story. He'd publish it, I'm sure."

"We don't have a story, Edward. We don't even have a witness right now." Harper tried not to sound angry. None of this was Edward's fault. Harper vented frustration on the hatch, twisting it open with a vicious jerk.

"Fine, then." Edward followed Harper through the hatch. "I give up. Where are we going?"

"Down." Harper smiled as he at last caught sight of the ladder he had been looking for. He tested his weight against its corroded iron rungs. It still held.

"Do you think you can climb one-handed?" Harper asked.

"I think so," Edward replied.

Harper went first. Edward followed. The phosphor lamp swung from side to side as Harper climbed. Its pale green light swept through the shadows of the ladder, casting patterns of crosses and rungs down into the darkness below. Distantly, Harper heard the hiss of steam pistons.

"You know, Waterstone used to have this theory that you were half-Prodigal," Edward said from above him.

"Really?" Harper snorted at the thought. "What in the name of God gave him that idea?"

"I think it started with the gloves."

"Hmm." Harper slowed his descent, realizing that the climb was harder for Edward than he would admit.

"You always seemed to be keeping something back. You know, all the other lads were so desperate to talk their heads off, and you never seemed to want to tell anyone anything. You always stood out that way. Waterstone was still rolling the idea around last time I talked to him. Not seriously. It just settled into a private joke between the two of us."

"I wish he were right," Harper replied. "Then I might have some Prodigal power to call on instead of just climbing down from here."

"Being able to fly would be rather handy right now, wouldn't it," Edward agreed.

The cut in Harper's palm throbbed each time he gripped a rung of the ladder. He glanced up to see how Edward was handling the climb. He moved slowly but smiled when he noticed Harper watching him.

"It's funny," Edward continued, "that Waterstone never said a thing about Joan."

"What?" Harper almost lost his grip. The lamp hanging from his forearm rocked wildly, flashing green light up into his face.

"He never suspected Joan, even though he met her dozens of times. She hid it so well, I don't think anyone would have suspected."

"How long have you known?" Harper asked.

"It took me a while to work the whole thing out. But after our honeymoon, I was pretty sure. There are some things that just can't be hidden when the two of you are...close."

"Why didn't you say anything?" Harper asked.

"I suppose I was waiting for her to confide in me." Edward shook his head. "If I had known how little time we would have together, I wouldn't have waited. It was so easy to imagine her being with me forever. I thought we had all the time in the world."

"I'm sorry." It was all Harper could say without betraying Joan's trust. He continued climbing down. He went slowly, making sure that Edward didn't fall too far behind him.

"I always wondered if you knew," Edward said. "I thought you did, but you never let on at all."

"If it had been my choice, I would have told you."

"I know."

They continued climbing. Harper couldn't think of anything to say. Edward always began their conversations, so Harper remained silent until Edward spoke again.

"I always wondered how you worked in the Inquisition and had a Prodigal sister at the same time." Edward's voice was quiet, almost tentative. He rarely spoke with such caution. Harper glanced up at him to see if something was wrong.

"You don't have to tell me if you don't feel like it," Edward said, catching Harper's curious glance.

"There's nothing much to tell. Joan never got into much trouble. The two halves of my life rarely crossed each other."

"I didn't mean directly." Edward paused as he shifted his arm awkwardly from one rung down to the next. "I guess I was wondering more about how you thought of Prodigals. On one hand you're a priest, and they are devils. On the other, your sister was one of them, and I know you loved her."

"I still do," Harper replied.

"Yes, I do too." Edward continued climbing in silence for several minutes. Harper said nothing. It seemed kinder to let Edward have his privacy. It was easier on Harper this way too. So long as Edward said nothing, Harper could not be tempted to comfort him with the truth.

But Harper knew the silence would not last. Edward had never been a private man. He had never had to disguise his desires as abstinence or crush his outrage to silence. Edward lived a life of shameless honesty.

"Isn't it strange," Edward said, "how you can know someone's gone, and yet you can't stop feeling as if they were still with you? Every Tuesday evening I still wander into the bedroom as if I need to remind her that the Pipers are going to be arriving for bridge. I know she's gone, but I don't quite feel it. I keep expecting to see her or hear her in the other room. At night when I'm just drifting off to sleep, I'll keep reaching out to put my arm around her..." Edward stopped for a few moments. "I'm sorry. I didn't mean to just keep rambling on."

"It's all right," Harper assured him. "People tend to ramble after they've been through an Inquisition confession. Talk all you want."

"Actually, I was hoping to hear you talk a little, Will. You never did say what you thought of Prodigals."

"You could pick another subject if you'd like," Harper offered.

"No. I want to know. I never could ask you before, but I want to know."

"The answer's not all that interesting." Harper peered down, but he still couldn't see to the end of their descent. The darkness below seemed infinite.

"Just tell me, and I'll decide if it's interesting or not," Edward said.

"Very well." Harper paused for a moment to think of how to put his thoughts into words. "The thing that I find absurd about condemning Prodigals as devils is that devils and angels are the same creatures. Prodigals were angels long before they were ever called devils. Lucifer, Satanel, Sariel, Azeal— all of them. Each of the fallen angels was created even before the earth, and they were not made from mud but from the will and body of God himself. Even the most degraded and ruined Prodigal is still closer to divinity than are any of us born of Adam's flesh."

"Is it just my ignorance, or does this opinion of yours smack of heresy?" Edward said after a moment.

"Yes, it does smack a little. But it's not just my opinion; it's stated fact in the scriptures. Lucifer, whom God made Prince of the Air and the Stars, is the same Lucifer who fell to the Abyss. Sariel and Rimmon were archangels of the storms before they became lords in hell. If we accept that Prodigals were once devils, then we must also acknowledge that they were also the third of Heaven's Host who revolted against God. They were angels. You can't have one without the other."

"I hadn't thought about it before, but I suppose you're right." After a moment Edward added, "It's amazing you haven't been excommunicated."

"I think you're the first person I've told." Harper glanced down again. There was a dim glow far below them. The sounds of the steam pistons grew steadily louder.

"Tell me." Edward had to raise his voice a little. "Do you live by the principle that what people don't know can't hurt them?"

"No," Harper replied. "What people don't know can't hurt me."

"Even better," Edward said. "So, do you have any other secret theories?"

"A few," Harper admitted.

"Well, tell me then."

"They're too dull. You'll nod off and fall off the ladder."

"You said the last one was uninteresting, and it shocked me quite a bit."

"Really?" Harper looked up to see if Edward was joking. Then he realized that he had been around Belimai too much lately. Edward was never sarcastic.

"Of course." Edward stopped to rest his arm, and Harper waited for him. "It's not every day that a captain of the Inquisition tells me he believes Prodigals are more divine than the Sons of Adam. Even radical anatomists like Raddly don't say things like that."

"The same Raddly who vomited in the deacon's urn?" Harper asked.

"Yes. He was barred from practice last year. Not because of the urn. As far as I know, no one has ever found out about that. Raddly published a paper revealing no differences between the bodies of baptized and unbaptized children. He drew the very unpopular conclusion that spiritual states might not affect physical bodies."

"Really? Did he use Prodigal children in any of his studies?" Harper asked.

"Yes." Edward began climbing again. "He didn't even try to publish that. He just happened to mention it to me when we were talking about the Prodigal murders that took place this spring. From the description of the remains, Raddly surmised that the killer was extracting the Prodigals' Ignis glands."

"For what little it's worth, he was right. They took the glands and blood to use in potions. They were making a huge profit from it." Harper was glad Edward couldn't see his face in the darkness. It still enraged him to think that his own abbot had been involved, and he still hated his own part in supplying Peter Roffcale for the slaughter.

"Joan was one of the victims, wasn't she?" Edward's voice sounded tight. "I guessed that you couldn't tell me because I wasn't supposed to know she was a Prodigal."

"I'm sorry, Edward." Harper's voice barely carried above the hisses and gasps of the steam pistons. "If I could go back and change things, I would."

"I know. I just wish it could have brought us closer instead of driving you off. I could have used the company, you know."

"I'm sorry." Harper wondered if he could ever stop saying he was sorry. He wondered if there would ever come a time when he had said it enough that it would make any difference.

"Did you catch the men who did it?" Edward asked.

"Yes and no," Harper replied. "The men who were abducting and murdering Prodigals are dead now. They were killed while resisting arrest. The men who assisted them and hid their activities are still free."

"If I ever found out who they were, I think I would murder them with my own hands." Edward's words were soft, but the anger in his voice ran deep.

Harper said nothing.

The chill of the shaft gave way to a moist heat. Light shot up through the grated walkway below him. He jumped down to the walkway. Only a few feet below, the steam pistons and water pumps roared and hissed as gallon after gallon of ore and water rolled through them.

The dirt and acid in the air stung Harper's skin and eyes. The smell of refuse and the sweat of Prodigal bodies hung on Harper's clothes like a mist. Edward coughed and weakly clambered down the last rungs of the ladder. His eyes watered and his light skin was already an irritated red.

"Where are we?" Edward asked.

"Hells Below," Harper replied. "We're a little east of the ore furnaces. We'll need to go west."

"Does the entire place burn like this?" Edward rubbed his eyes.

"Yes. You'll get used to it. Once you're inside, it'll be a little better."

Harper studied Edward. His rough, gray cell clothes would have stood out horribly anywhere else, but in Hells Below many people had been held by the Inquisition. Few of them were wealthy enough to throw away the clothes they were issued on release. Harper's own appearance would be far more remarkable.

"We'll trade pants." Harper decided. "You can take my vest as well. It'll look like you've been out for a while that way."

Harper quickly stripped off his pants and vest, then handed them to Edward. Edward fumbled with the buttons of his pants with his uninjured hand. Harper removed the Inquisition insignias from the collar of his coat. He removed the priest's collar from his shirt as well.

Edward stepped out of his baggy, gray trousers with an awkward shyness. Harper found it hard not to steal a glance at Edward's bare waist and legs. At one time he had been very attracted to Edward. But that had been long before Edward became his brother-in-law. What remained of Harper's desire after Edward became his brother was a deep affection and slight curiosity. Harper kept his eyes to himself.

Harper snatched up Edward's discarded pants and busied himself tucking in his white shirt while Edward dressed.

"All part of my new, criminal life, I suppose," Edward said as he straightened Harper's vest over his shirt. "How do I look?"

Nervous, Harper thought, but he didn't say so. Instead he smiled.

"You should wear my clothes more often. You look good in black."

"So, what now?" Edward asked.

"Now you go to a safe house."

"A safe house?" Edward asked. "A safe house from the Inquisition? Are there really such things?"

"A few." Harper turned and strode quickly along the walkway. Before Edward could question him further, Harper took a sharp turn and swung down the emergency stairs to the ground of Hells Below.

He led Edward through the narrow streets. Decaying houses and rumpled, dark shops jutted into the streets and hunched against each other like drunks.

"They're going to ask you what the Inquisition wants you for," Harper said quietly. "Don't tell them. Just say that you're a physician looking for work. There aren't any doctors down here. You're worth more than any reward. They'll sell their own kids before they'll turn you over to the Inqu—"

"Will, you're coming with me, aren't you?" Edward broke in. Oily droplets of condensation spattered down from the cavernous roof and drummed across the roofs of the crumbling houses. Harper and Edward walked under the cover of the overhanging eaves.

"You'll be fine," Harper began.

"No. You don't understand." Edward glanced askance to see if any one was near enough to overhear them.

Three Prodigal boys played with a nest of rats at the far end of the alley, but none of them took any note of either Harper or Edward.

"Will, it isn't going to be safe for you in the city. They made me sign a confession. I didn't want to, but—"

"I know. I went through the files and pulled it out."

"You did?" Edward looked a little startled. "How did you know?"

"That's just how the Inquisition works. They get confessions and then use them to bargain for trial testimonies."

"Are you angry?"

"Not with you. You did the smart thing. Hell, you did the only thing you could. If you hadn't given them that confession, they wouldn't have stopped torturing you. You wouldn't have been in any shape to escape when I came for you." Harper frowned. "I'm just sorry I didn't get you out sooner. I shouldn't have left you the way I did."

"You had someone else to look after." Edward shrugged. "Did you take care of him?"

"We need to take Wax Street." Harper pointed ahead.

"You could be less obvious about not answering, you know," Edward said as they continued on.

"You see that little chapel." Harper inclined his head toward the brick building. "That's where you're going. You'll want to talk to Bastard Jack."

"Not his real name, I hope," Edward commented.

"You never know with Prodigals. It doesn't matter. Just ask for him, and tell him that Nick Sariel recommended him to you."

"What if this Nick Sariel is there?"

"He's locked up at Brighton," Harper said. "Just drop his name if they ask. What's going to interest Jack is the fact that you're a physician. Once he knows that, he'll piss himself to make a friend of you. The only other thing you have to remember is not to mention me, not to anyone down here. Inquisition captains are never popular, and neither are their friends." Harper patted him on the shoulder, then stepped back. "You think you've got all that?"

"Yes, but—"

"Good. Take care of yourself, Edward."

"Will—"

"Just say goodbye," Harper told him as coldly as he could.

"Goodbye."

"Goodbye."

Harper turned before Edward could say anything more and walked away. He didn't want to drag this out, and he didn't want to discuss it. The less time Edward spent in his company, the better chance he had. Harper knew Edward was watching his retreating back.

Only after he knew he was well out of Edward's sight did he turn back. He dashed back to the wooden fire escape that was nailed to the back of a rotting tenement. Two of the steps snapped under Harper's weight, but the rest of the ladder held. He climbed up onto the roof and looked across to Wax Street. Through the haze of falling condensation, Harper watched as Edward slowly approached the brick chapel and then disappeared inside.

Though there was no day or night in Hells Below, it felt suddenly much darker to Harper.

Chapter Nine
Silk Stocking

*H*arper wanted to think calmly. He wanted to feel that familiar, detached coldness enfold the burning rage inside him, but it wouldn't come. He didn't know why. Perhaps it had been seeing Edward hunched in that cell, too frightened to even look up. Or Joan, dressed like beggar and covered in filth, staring at him as if he might harm her. Perhaps it had been holding Belimai's shaking body in his arms and knowing that nothing could ever give Belimai his innocence back. Or perhaps it was simply remembering all those things and looking out over the desolation of Hells Below. The injustice seemed infinite. Fury welled up through Harper.

He had spent years gathering evidence and following the correct procedures of prosecution. All the while, Abbot Greeley and his friends committed brutal crimes whenever they pleased and had witnesses murdered at their leisure. Time after time, Harper had crushed his own anger and poured his strength into the belief that justice had to prevail.

But justice did not prevail. It struggled, floundered, then sank into oblivion.

Harper had been told as a child that God brought Justice to every man. Harper had believed that. Even as his innocence fell from his body, even as he uncovered mutilated women and gutted Prodigals, Harper had clung to that promise. Now he couldn't make himself believe it any longer. No wide-eyed saint or righteous angel was going to give Harper Justice. He didn't even want it any longer.

What he wanted now was vengeance. For that, he did not have to wait on heaven's judgment. Vengeance he could take with his own hands. It wasn't smart. Harper knew that, but he didn't care. His life was already in ruins.

When Harper had left Hells Below, the drops of condensation clung to his hair and skin like baptismal waters. His anger cooled as he walked, but it didn't fade. By the time he reached the open air of Champion Street, he'd already decided on a course of action. He made his way through the dark streets to Cherry Row and up into one of the squalid little flats.

Now, he watched from the grimy window as a single figure strode across the street below. Only a few of the streetlamps had been repaired since the deluge the week before. This particular little road had only one working lamp. Harper smiled as he caught the shine of red hair under the light.

Harper pulled the curtains closed and walked carefully across the small, dark room to the door.

"Not much longer, now," Harper whispered to the woman on the bed.

She stared at him with wide, terrified eyes. She didn't even attempt a reply through the wadded-up cloth and silk stocking that Harper had used to gag her. The deadness to her responses told Harper that he was not the first man to treat her this way. She hadn't tried to cry for help. She had already known that no one would respond to the screams of a whore. She hadn't even struggled against Harper's strength when he slammed her down onto the bed and tied her. She lay still, giving Harper no reason to hurt her, no resistance to beat down. She just watched him, with an expression of hopeless knowing.

"This will all be over soon," Harper said quietly. "Just stay where you are, and you'll be fine."

She nodded slightly. Through the darkness, Harper smiled at her.

The sounds of footsteps on the stairs grew louder. Keys jingled like bells as Brandson tried to find the right one. At last the door swung open. Brandson stepped inside and groped for the wall lamp. The door fell shut behind him. Harper silently twisted the lock back into place.

"I'm not paying you to be asleep, Lucy." Brandson kept fiddling with the lamp. "I've had a hell of a day, and it's going to take more than a drowsy hand job to make it better."

A weak flame flickered up into the dirty, glass housing of the lamp. Brandson lost his grip on his coat as he suddenly saw Lucy.

"What the hell is this?" Brandson demanded.

Stepping up from behind, Harper pushed the barrel of his pistol hard against the back of Brandson's neck.

"This is where your day gets even worse," Harper said. "You know the procedure, Captain. Arms up. Do anything else, and I'll spatter Lucy, over there, with the majority of your head." Harper reached under Brandson's raised arm and removed Brandson's pistol. He pocketed it.

"Very good." Harper ran his hand down to Brandson's waist and unbuckled his belt. Years of desperate encounters in back alleys had made the motion second nature to him. He unclipped the handcuffs from the belt and then let Brandson's belt and pants fall to the floor. A shudder of fear and protest moved through Brandson's body.

"Keep your hands up," Harper snapped when he felt the slight shift in Brandson's shoulders. Brandson jerked his arms back up.

"I never appreciated how well you followed orders until now," Harper commented. "Left arm behind your back."

Brandson did as Harper told him.

"Now the right." Harper cuffed Brandson's hands behind his back tightly.

"Now, slowly down onto your knees." Harper pressed the pistol down against Brandson's skin as Brandson sank to his knees. Harper kept his pistol snug against Brandson as he reached down and jerked the belt out from the folds of cloth around Brandson's ankles. Harper's right palm ached as he moved his hand. The cut split open again. The sharp pain only made him angrier at Brandson.

Harper wrapped the belt around Brandson's ankles, pulling it tight with vicious jerks, and then buckled it. The black leather cut into the muscle of Brandson's legs. Brandson winced. Harper stepped back and then kicked him forward onto his stomach. He hit the floor with a hard thud.

Harper crouched down near Brandson's face.

"So, Captain, why do you think I'm here?" Harper asked.

"Your brother-in-law, Dr. Talbott," Brandson muttered against the floor. "I can get him a full exoneration if that's what—"

"Don't pretend to bargain with me." Harper grabbed a fistful of Brandson's red hair and jerked his face up close to his own. "Right now I want to kill you so badly it hurts, so don't give me a reason. Just answer my questions. Understand?"

"Yes," Brandson whispered. Harper released his hair and Brandson's head dropped back down to the floor.

"Who killed the woman Dr. Talbott was treating?"

"The abbot gave direct orders—"

"I said, who killed her?" Harper demanded.

"There were three of us."

"You were the one who put the bullet through her, weren't you?" Harper rested the muzzle of his pistol against the base of Brandson's skull. Brandson squeezed his eyes shut and nodded his head against the floor in silent admission.

"Who were the other two?" Harper asked.

"Captain Spencer and Captain Warren."

"What about Reynolds and Miller?" Harper asked.

"No, the abbot hates them. He thinks they're filthy sodomites."

"I see." Harper stood and then rolled Brandson over with his foot. He stared down at Brandson's pale face.

"It was the abbot's order. I had to do it, Harper," Brandson whispered. "Her testimony would have convicted Lord Cedric. It would have been a huge scandal."

"Didn't it even occur to you that Lord Cedric deserves to be convicted? He murdered his niece."

"He never meant to. She fell down the stairs—"

"Her body was covered with months of bruises, Brandson. He was beating her, and she died trying to escape him. Anyone who bothered to look at her could have seen that." Harper crouched down beside Brandson, pressing the tip of his gun against Brandson's chest. "If you fell down a flight of stairs trying to escape me, don't you think I might be to blame for your death?"

Brandson stared at Harper in silence for several moments. Harper didn't know what Brandson saw in his expression, but suddenly Brandson squeezed his eyes shut.

"Don't kill me, Harper. I'll...I'll do what ever you want. Just don't kill me."

Harper looked away in disgust as Brandson begged. He took a deep breath of the cool air.

"Just answer my questions, Brandson," Harper said.

"I will, I swear."

"Where is the abbot keeping Lord Cedric?" Harper asked.

"I'm not supposed to—"

Harper cocked the hammer of his pistol.

"White Chapel!" Brandson shouted. Sweat poured down his forehead. "For the love of God, don't kill me, Harper. Please..."

Slowly, Harper released the hammer. Then he stood up and went to Lucy. She stared at the pistol in his hand, then glanced up at his face. Harper gave her a brief smile. She tried to return the smile, but she was too frightened to be convincing. The gag in her mouth made the expression grotesquely desperate.

Harper sighed and strode quickly to the woman's shabby dressing table. He opened the drawer and dug through her underwear until he found another pair of silk stockings. There was a little pattern of L's decorating the seams. He took those as well as a pair of underwear and a cotton sock.

Harper returned to Brandson. He holstered his pistol and then viciously yanked him up off the floor and shoved him back onto the bed. Brandson gave and absurd cry of surprise. Lucy bounced as the mattress heaved with Brandson's sudden weight.

Harper didn't wait for Brandson to gain his equilibrium. He grabbed Brandson's legs and lashed them to the iron rungs at the foot of the bed. Then Harper sat on Brandson's chest, pinning his cuffed arms under his back. He tied one end of a silk stocking around Brandson's throat like a leash and then knotted the other end to the headboard.

"Open your mouth," Harper commanded, and Brandson obeyed.

Harper shoved the underwear into Brandson's mouth, cramming them in until he gagged. He used the remaining cotton sock to hold them in place. After briefly checking his knots, Harper got off him. He walked around the bed and, much more gently, untied Lucy's arms and legs.

He led her by one arm as he picked up Brandson's coat and keys, and then left the room. He stopped in the hallway with her.

"I'm going to take your gag off. But you have to stay quiet," Harper told her.

Lucy nodded. Harper untied the gag, taking care not to pull her hair. When he did, she winced but made no noise. At last Harper pulled the stocking off, and Lucy spit out the wet wad of cloth that had been in her mouth. The sides of her face were red from the tightness of the gag.

"I'm going to let you go," Harper told her. "But you should leave the city if you can. This will help." Harper pulled Brandson's wallet and coin purse out of the coat. Lucy reached out tentatively and took the money.

"You might think of going to the Inquisition to report this," Harper said, "but you should remember that it was an abbot who ordered Brandson to kill another woman for knowing what you just heard. Do you understand me?"

"Yes," she whispered quickly.

"He wasn't kind to you, was he?" Harper asked suddenly, remembering how resigned she had been to the bonds and gag.

"Worse than some, better than others." She looked up at Harper. "Can I have his coat? I haven't got one of my own."

"Here." Harper handed it to her.

"Thank you." She put the big black coat on and then headed down the stairs. Harper watched her go.

"Good luck," Harper told her as she turned away. Lucy glanced back up at him.

"Good luck to you too," she said, and then she rushed into the darkness.

Harper turned back to the door. He was glad to have let Lucy go. She was the kind of girl who had seen too many ugly things already. He wouldn't have wanted her to witness what he had left to do with Brandson.

Chapter Ten
Crooked Teeth

*T*he sun had risen an hour ago, but the sky remained dim. Heavy gray clouds hung above the rooftops and wrapped the tall steeples in thick mist. Harper liked the fog. It suited his thoughts, disguised the stains on his clothing, and hid his features. As the city bells rang out the hour, Harper squinted up the street.

Vendors were already out hawking their goods. Carriages and cart horses tore deep grooves through the muddy roads as the drivers shouted each other aside. The smell of hot bread and piss mixed as bakers opened their doors and women emptied the previous night's chamber pots into the gutters.

Harper sidestepped a splash of fouled water. His stomach clenched at the smell. He had already walked from Lucy's rented rooms on Cherry Row to Brandson's house on Archer's Green Road, then made his way to the walled grounds of White Chapel. Now he strode back along Butcher Street. The muscles of his back and legs burned with exhaustion. His eyes ached from strain and fatigue. His stomach churned in a mixture of hunger and tension. He felt almost certain that the moment he stopped moving he would simply collapse.

"Captain!" a young man shouted.

Across the street, a dark haired youth beckoned him.

"Captain." The young man grinned and Harper recognized him. Harper didn't know anyone else with so many teeth crammed so wildly into his mouth. Harper waved a brief hello. The young man returned the gesture with clumsy enthusiasm.

"Come across, Captain," the young man shouted over an argument between two carriage drivers. Harper waited for a slow moment in the rolling advances of carts and carriages, then rushed across the street.

"Morris," Harper said. "What are you doing down here?"

"Working." The young man held up a dripping broom. "Can you believe it?"

"Street sweeping?" Harper frowned.

"No. I'm just cleaning up in front of the shop." He pointed up to the sign that hung over their heads. Harper glanced up at the painted image of a loaf of bread encircled by patterns of wheat leaves.

"I got an apprenticeship to a baker." Morris pointed to the stained apron he wore. "Mr. Stone's been showing me how to make butter pastries. I baked my first ones this morning."

"That's good. I'm glad things have worked out for you." Harper smiled. Sharp tremors of exhaustion passed through his legs as he continued standing. If he didn't get moving again, he thought he was going to drop.

Morris beamed at him, his riot of Prodigal teeth flashing out again from behind his lips.

"You wouldn't have thought it could happen, would you? You would have thought I'd be back to doing light work out of other folks' pockets, wouldn't you?" Morris bounced slightly on the balls of his feet in excitement. Just watching him made the bones of Harper's feet ache.

"Well, you were quite good at it," Harper replied.

"That is all too true. Even Sister Celeste said there was no honest work for a yellow-eyed bastard like me." Morris swept the broom across the store steps, splashing the puddles of water aside. "But Mr. Stone says, such is not the case. He says it like that too. 'My lad, such is not the case.'"

"Well, congratulations." Harper patted Morris' shoulder and started to turn away.

"Captain, would you come in and meet Mr. Stone? I told him all about you and how you kept dragging me back to the charity school. He said if I saw you again, I should have you into the shop so he could thank you." Morris leaned a little closer to Harper. "Mr. Stone will probably give you some free grub."

"Well..."

Morris looked entreating. It clearly meant a great deal to him to have Harper meet the good Mr. Stone. In any case, Harper thought, having food in his stomach could hardly do him any harm.

"I can't stay long," Harper told Morris.

"Mr. Stone will be so pleased."

"Lead on, then," Harper replied.

He followed Morris into the red brick building. The warmth of the bakery made Harper feel suddenly more tired. The room smelled of yeast and vanilla. A big man with a black beard and thick black hair looked up as Harper and Morris entered.

"Mr. Stone. This is the captain I was telling you about." Morris gestured to Harper.

Mr. Stone frowned slightly as he regarded Harper. Harper knew he looked bad. He hadn't shaved, and his clothes were stained with both oil from Hells Below and mud. He didn't come close to presenting the proper image of an Inquisition captain.

"I imagined you'd be older," Mr. Stone said after a moment.

Harper shrugged.

"Pleased to meet you, in any case." Mr. Stone held out his hand and Harper shook it. Mr. Stone's hand was hot and callused. "You look like you could use something to eat."

"Thank you. That would be quite kind."

"Would you like a butter pastry?" Morris asked.

"Give the man two, lad," Mr. Stone said before Harper could answer. "Make sure they're good and cool first. And check on the beef pies while you're at it." Mr. Stone tossed an oven mitt to Morris. Morris caught it and then darted through a curtained doorway just behind Mr. Stone. A hot billow of air rolled out as the curtains swung behind him. Harper guessed the ovens were back there. His eyes drooped almost closed as the new wave of heat wafted over him.

He didn't think he had been this warm in days.

"I hope you don't mind me saying so," Mr. Stone said to Harper, "but you look dead on your feet."

"I was on my way to bed when Morris saw me," Harper replied. Mr. Stone continued to study Harper curiously. Harper decided to redirect the conversation before Mr. Stone could ask any difficult questions.

"It really is kind of you to take Morris on," Harper said. "Most men wouldn't want a Prodigal in their shops, much less working for them."

"Well, I wouldn't want most of them," Mr. Stone replied. "But I can say the same for most of the natural men I know as well. I think Morris was meant to be a baker."

Harper didn't know if it was his exhaustion or the seriousness of Mr. Stone's tone, but it made him want to laugh. The last thing he would have thought of Morris was that he was born to bake. Not with those teeth. Harper had a jagged scar on his forearm from the first time he had encountered Morris.

"The heat," Mr. Stone continued, "it gets most men. Hurts their eyes and makes their skin crack. Wears them down, but not Morris. He looks as rosy as a cherub after a whole day back there. He takes to the work better than my own son ever did, I'll tell you that."

"That's good. I'm glad Morris has found an honest living." Harper straightened as he realized that he'd been slumping over Mr. Stone's counter.

"But you see, Captain." Mr. Stone dropped his voice. "There's trouble with him taking to it so well."

There was something about the low whisper that grabbed Harper's attention.

"How do you mean?" Harper asked.

"My own boy hasn't been good for anything. He doesn't work and he doesn't give a damn about the shop. He thinks he's going to sell the place when I die."

Harper frowned slightly, not at the thought of Mr. Stone or his unruly son, but simply at the idea that he was getting dragged into their business. Harper had more than enough troubles of his own at the moment.

"This bakery's been in the family since my great-great grandfather's days," Mr. Stone went on. "It doesn't just belong to the family; it's what our family is built on. I don't want him selling it. I want Morris to run it after I'm gone, but legally—"

"It will belong to your son?" Harper finished.

"Yes. That's the short of it."

"Well, if you're set on keeping the shop from your son, then you can disinherit him."

"No, I couldn't do that. He's no good, but he's still my son."

"Your only other choice is to adopt Morris and will the bakery to him. Your natural son couldn't contest it, if Morris was also legally your son."

"Can that be done?" Mr. Stone asked. "I've never heard of it."

"There's no law barring it," Harper replied. "So long as you didn't mind making Morris your son..."

"I get on with him better than the real one, I'll tell you that. I'd have done it a year ago if I knew I could." Mr. Stone smiled for the first time, and Harper noted that the man's teeth were nearly as crooked as Morris'. "I thought a man of the law might have an answer for me," Mr. Stone told Harper. "That's why I said to Morris that he should have you in next time he saw you. I'm sorry for keeping you from your bed, though."

"I'm just a little tired." Harper forced his bloodshot eyes open wide.

"Hey, Morris!" Mr. Stone suddenly shouted.

"Yes, sir?" Morris yelled from the back rooms.

"The captain is going to be asleep on his feet if you take any longer."

"I'm just cutting the bread. I'll be up before you can say your grace."

"Your grace," Mr. Stone said under his breath.

"Very funny, Mr. Stone." Morris pushed the curtains aside with his shoulder as he came into the front room carrying a wax paper bag in one hand and a steaming tray of beef pies in the other.

"This is for you, Captain." Morris handed him the bag.

"Thank you." Harper could smell the sweet buttery pastries even through the parchment wrapped around them.

Morris grinned and spun the baking tray in his hand.

"We've also got customers coming in, Morris." Mr. Stone took the tray from Morris and slid it into the rack of savory pies.

A gust of cold wetness tumbled in through the door as two nuns rushed in. They were followed by small pack of schoolboys in red uniforms.

They all seemed so familiar with Morris. The old nun teased him harmlessly, returning his ragged smile with her own toothless one. Harper suddenly thought that Mr. Stone was right. Morris did seem to belong here.

For a moment he wondered if this was the kind of life that Belimai might have led if he had never been tortured by the Inquisition. Harper tried to imagine Belimai smiling sweetly at a nun. Harper shook his head. He really was delirious from exhaustion if he thought Belimai would have ever done that.

Harper opened the door and scowled at the frigid air that swept in.

"God bless you, Captain," Morris called after him.

"Take good care," Harper replied.

He trudged up Butcher Street making silent promises to his shivering, tired body. Six more blocks, and there would be a bed. Just six more blocks to a warm, soft bed.

At last he stumbled up the narrow staircase like a drunk. Belimai's rooms were cold. Wind and rain swept in through the broken windows. Little had changed in the two weeks since he'd last been here. Belimai's desk still lay on its side, surrounded by fallen books and crumpled drawings. The cracked syringes lay where Belimai had thrown them.

Once Sariel had been arrested for the murder of Lord Cedric's niece, there hadn't been any reason for the Inquisition to keep looking for Belimai. One Prodigal was as good as another, as far as they were concerned.

Harper knew he, himself, was another matter. From both Sariel's and Edward's confessions, he knew that the abbot wanted to bring him in specifically. He realized that he was the one remaining person who posed a threat to the abbot and Lord Cedric. Knowing what they had done to the old woman, Harper had no illusions as to what the abbot intended for him. Inquisitors would be waiting for him at his townhouse.

Eventually nowhere would be safe for him, not so long as the abbot had power.

Harper took the papers out of his pocket and read over them one more time. Slowly, he went to the wreck of Belimai's desk and picked up a gum eraser. He quickly lifted off the notes the abbot had made on Sariel's confession. What remained was usable. The few details it mentioned matched the confession he had forced Brandson to write.

Harper felt slightly sick, thinking of Brandson. Or perhaps it was exhaustion. He slipped the papers back into his pocket.

Harper staggered to the bedroom and dropped the bag Morris had given him down onto the bedside. Then he flopped down onto the thin mattress. He didn't even bother to take off his boots. He simply fell asleep.

Feverish, splintered images crashed through his dreams. Harper rolled and tossed, twisting the blankets and his clothes. The heavy cloth seemed to pull and shift around him. Suddenly, something icy gripped his leg and jerked at it. Harper kicked hard and bolted upright. His hand clamped around the butt of his pistol before he even took in his surroundings.

Belimai glared at him from where he had been knocked to the floor. He had one of Harper's boots in his hand.

"Last time I do you any favors." Belimai stood and then tossed the boot aside.

"What in God's name are you doing here?" Harper's voice was rough from sleep. His thoughts still foundered in the confused wake of his dreams.

"I live here," Belimai quipped. He pulled off his own shoes and sat down across from Harper on the bed.

"I wasn't sure if it would be safe to come back, so I was watching for Inquisitors from the roof across the street. Then I saw you just wander in past the open windows and plop down on the bed."

"You're supposed to be back at the estate house," Harper said.

"As I recall, so are you." Belimai slipped his legs under the blankets. His knee just touched Harper's thigh. He leaned back against the footboard of the bed and gazed at Harper. "What was so urgent that you had to rush off without saying anything?"

"Edward needed my help." Harper shifted a little closer to Belimai. He was cold, but it felt good to touch him. It was comforting for no good reason except that Harper hadn't been able to do it in days.

"Your blonde brother-in-law got in trouble?" Belimai's eyes narrowed slightly. "So, off you race to his rescue. How very gallant you are, Captain Harper. Does he still need you?"

"He's safe for now, but probably not very happy." Harper worked his remaining boot off, then kicked it out from under the blankets. "Where's Joan?"

"She dashed off to find you after two Inquisition captains came around the estate house looking for you. Captain Spencer and another Captain Warner or Warr—"

"Warren," Harper supplied.

"Yes, that was the name. So, you already knew." Belimai shrugged "In any case, your sister said she had to go warn you. She's looking for you in Hells Below, I think."

"She just left you?" Harper demanded.

"Yes. She seemed to believe me when I told her I was a grown man and could look after myself," Belimai replied. "And in any case, the habit seems to run in your family. You did the same thing." Belimai jabbed one of his long toes against Harper's stomach. "I'm amazed you don't have to get up now and save some orphan or find a missing dog."

"I'm sorry I left you, Belimai, but Edward was taken in by the Inquisition because of me. I had to get him out of there. You of all people should understand that."

"Oh, I understand. I just don't like it." Belimai jabbed Harper in the stomach two more times. Harper grabbed Belimai's bony foot and jerked him down flat on his back.

"Are you jealous? Am I only allowed to save you?" Harper pounced on top of Belimai, pinning him against the bed.

"You really can be an overbearing ass sometimes, you know that?" Belimai glared up at him.

"Yes, I know." Harper leaned forward so that his lips brushed Belimai's. "But you find me charming anyway, don't you?" Harper smiled and waited for Belimai's scathing reply. Instead he received a sharp jab in the side. Harper winced.

"I'm too tired to be clever, so you'll just have to settle for that," Belimai said.

"So, what exactly does a broken rib mean?" Harper asked.

"A broken rib." Belimai raised a black brow. "I hardly touched you."

"More's the pity." Harper leaned down again and kissed Belimai lightly on the lips. He felt Belimai's breath catch as they touched. Harper pulled back just enough to see Belimai's eyes close, then flash open again.

Belimai returned Harper's stare with a hard focus that he had never had before. The soft, drugged languor that Harper had grown so used to was gone. Belimai watched him with a starved intensity. His hands curled across Harper's back and pulled him back down. Belimai's tongue darted between Harper's lips, both invading and inviting. There was a ferocity to the kiss that seared through Harper. He forgot his gentle intentions and train of conversation.

With rough desperation, Harper pulled Belimai's loose clothes off. He ran his hands across the naked expanse of pale skin, savoring each hollow and curve. Belimai's hands slid under Harper's shirt and skimmed across his nipples. Then, with agonizing care, Belimai stroked the line of Harper's belt.

He kissed Harper again. Their tongues thrust and twined. Harper's entire body tensed. He kissed Belimai's throat, chest, and hips. His teeth grazed Belimai's arching flesh. Harper lifted his head and kissed Belimai's mouth, passing the taste of his own skin back to him.

Belimai pulled Harper's pants open. His hands curled around Harper. As if kneeling in prayer, Belimai bowed down and took Harper into the soft heat of his mouth. Harper's breath came in fast gasps. Harper's hips rocked with rushes of pleasure. He forced the sharp thrusts back into gentle motions. His muscles ached from restraint and driving desire.

Slowly, Harper turned and shifted around Belimai to recip-rocate. Belimai moved with him, never lifting his head. They curled around each other, mirroring thrusts, sucking, and arching against each other in a driving rhythm. Shocks of pleasure jolted through Harper's body as Belimai swallowed him deeply.

Harper drew Belimai's hips closer. Ravenous, Harper sucked at Belimai, exulting in the mounting speed of Belimai's response. Harper's own body already raged beyond his control. Belimai's thrusts quickened, and Harper matched him. They moved to-gether, their bodies locked in desperate motion and exquisite pleasure.

Ecstasy burst through Harper's body. It washed through his bones, blood, and muscles. It engulfed him in a thoughtless pu-rity far deeper than even sleep. Harper lost himself—every fear, rage, hope, and desire—in a flood of physical joy.

Then the moment passed. Harper felt utterly exhausted. He managed to turn around and drape one arm over Belimai's spent body. He could hardly keep his eyes open as he pressed a kiss against Belimai's lips. Belimai shifted against him and pulled the blankets over them both.

"All right," Belimai whispered so softly that Harper hardly heard him, "I do find you charming."

Chapter Eleven
Liar

When Harper awoke, he was alone in the bed. The dull light of a few streetlamps poured in through the broken windows. Twilight winds tumbled through the torn curtains, carrying fat droplets of rain inside. Harper looked around the room and caught the outline of Belimai's thin body. Belimai moved cautiously. He held his shoes in his hands as he pulled on a coat. Then he crept toward the door, stepping expertly past the floorboards that might have groaned or creaked.

"Where are you going?" Harper asked.

Belimai spun back on him.

"Out for a walk," Belimai said.

"It's raining." Harper sat up. A chill hung through the room.

"I need to stretch my legs a little." Belimai took another step toward the door.

"I'll go with you."

Belimai's secretiveness worried Harper. It seemed utterly at odds with the way he had behaved only a few hours ago. Harper grabbed his scattered clothes from the floor. He pulled on his pants. The cloth was unpleasantly cold and still damp from the morning rain.

"Harper, don't," Belimai said. "Don't come with me."

"Why shouldn't I?" Harper already had his suspicion.

"You need to get more sleep."

"I'm already up." Harper forced a smile. "Try again."

"I would just rather do some things by myself." Belimai's voice was oddly soft.

"Are you going to look for ophorium?" Harper quickly crossed the space between them. He should have guessed that Belimai would be tempted to feed his addiction once he returned to the capital.

Belimai turned to Harper and looked directly at him. Up close, Harper could see the strange expression on Belimai's face. His eyes were wide and oddly shiny. He pressed his lips closed, drawing quick breaths in through his flared nostrils. Belimai had worn the same expression after Mr. Scott-Beck had nearly gutted him. Seeing it again, now, alarmed Harper.

"Most men are tempted to go back to it." Harper tried to draw the accusation out of his previous words. "It's a hard thing to give up. Normally, people slip a few times before they can make a clean break."

Belimai said nothing, just stared at him. It wasn't like Belimai to be so quiet or to look so fragile after a mere remark. There was something more to this, Harper knew. But he didn't know what.

"Look, Belimai. I know how hard this has to—"

"Be quiet." Belimai held up his hand. "I'm not going out searching for a fix." Slowly, he drew back from Harper. "I'm going to the Inquisition."

"What?" Harper could hardly put breath behind his voice.

"I have to turn myself over to them. We both know it," Belimai said.

Harper thought that someone might have shoved a steel blade into his guts. A shocking, hard pain wrenched through him. He stared at Belimai in stunned horror for a moment. His sister must have told Belimai about Sariel. There couldn't be any other reason that Belimai would turn himself in.

"You can't do that." Harper grabbed Belimai, knocking the shoes from his hands. "Why can't you just forget about him? All he's ever done is ruin your life!"

"What are you talking about?" Belimai stared at him.

"You and Sariel." Harper knew his voice was rising with rage, but he couldn't seem to stop it. "Do you think I'm just going to let it happen all over again?"

"Harper, have you gone mad?" Belimai asked.

"You aren't going to turn yourself in for Sariel," Harper stated flatly.

"I was never going to, you idiot," Belimai snapped. "I'm doing this for you."

"What?" Harper's anger and pain dropped into an abyss of confusion.

"I ought to jab you in the eye for making me have to say it out loud," Belimai growled.

"You can jab me anywhere you like; just explain what you're talking about."

Belimai glared at him, but Harper found the expression almost reassuring after that strange, wide-eyed look Belimai had given him earlier.

"You did say you were turning yourself in to the Inquisition…" Harper spoke with slow deliberation, watching Belimai's face with each word.

"I didn't say anything about Sariel. Why did you bring him up?"

"Why else would you want to turn yourself in?" Harper brushed past Belimai's question.

"Sariel's not even—" Belimai cut himself off as a realization came to him. "He's been arrested, hasn't he?"

"Joan didn't tell you?" Harper asked.

"No."

"Then why were you going to the Inquisition?"

"You're an idiot, aren't you?" Belimai demanded.

"Yes, I am. So, tell me why you were going to the Inquisition."

"Because of you, you moron," Belimai said. "Look at what I've already done to you. You're tired and filthy. You can't go home. The Inquisition is hunting for you. You're a mess from trying to protect me."

"So, you were going to turn yourself in for my sake?" The idea was touching, but also terrible. Harper knew he couldn't have lived with himself if he had been the reason Belimai turned himself over to the Inquisition.

"I wouldn't be doing it for my own sake. Of course it would be for you." Belimai scowled.

"Don't even think about it, Belimai." Harper shook his head. "Do you think I could stand it if—"

"If what? If you finally got rid of a pathetic junkie? That would be a shame, wouldn't it?"

"No. You know that isn't how I think of you."

"Weren't you just accusing me of going out to find a fix? Wasn't that you, Captain Harper?" Belimai forced his mouth into a smile, trying to look as if he took pleasure in proving his point. "You know, you're not fooling anyone but yourself. You know I'm trash. You wouldn't have a use for me any other way, would you? You need some crust of Prodigal shit to rescue so you can feel like a savior. So you can sacrifice yourself. Who knows, if you could get yourself killed, someone might even decide to make you a saint."

Harper opened his mouth to tell Belimai that he was wrong, but Belimai went on in a rush.

"Well, fuck you!" Tiny rivulets of blood seeped from Belimai's eyes. "I don't want to be saved. I don't want you to be my personal martyr. I'm going to turn myself in and save you."

"You can't." Harper's words came out in a tight whisper. He swallowed and felt as if he were drinking shattered glass.

"Like hell I can't." Belimai snatched up one of his shoes and looked around to find the other. "We'll see how you like being the reason a man loses everything, you perfect bastard. Where is my goddamn shoe?"

"It won't do me any good if you turn yourself over," Harper said quietly. "The Inquisition isn't after you anymore. They never were. You just fit the description of the Prodigal they needed. They found someone else."

Belimai stood there, caught in a paralyzed flux of rage and uncertainty. At last he hurled his shoe at Harper. The heel smacked across the corner of Harper's shoulder. He hardly registered the blow.

"I'm sorry, Belimai." Harper sat back down on the edge of the bed. "They arrested Sariel when they couldn't find you."

"They took Sariel?" Belimai asked quietly.

"There are only a few of you in the entire city who can fly, and the Inquisition only has records of you and Sariel. It was bound to be one or the other of you."

"So once they had Sariel, I no longer mattered. You aren't in trouble for hiding me?" Belimai asked.

"That first night was dangerous, but after that, no." Harper wanted to say something more, but all that came out were cold statements of fact. He sounded like he was giving a court testimony.

"Why were those two captains looking for you?" Belimai crossed his arms over his chest. "Have you found a new lost cause? Your sister, your brother-in-law, some bad dog?"

Harper leaned down to where his wet coat lay in a heap. He dug through the pockets and pulled out the papers he had stolen. He handed them to Belimai.

"I'm not the good Inquisitor that you like to imagine me to be, Belimai."

"No?" Belimai glanced between the papers and Harper. "Aren't you the man who wants to redeem every living Prodigal?"

"No." The slicing pain in Harper's throat cut his voice to a thin breath. "I've never wanted to redeem you. I wanted to join you."

Belimai's brow wrinkled. Harper knew Belimai couldn't understand how he could want such a thing. For Belimai, Prodigal blood was nothing but a curse. Belimai looked down at the papers as if he could find an explanation there. He read intently. Harper watched Belimai's frown deepen into a scowl. At last, Belimai folded the confessions and handed them back to Harper.

"Have you done any of these things?" Belimai asked.

"No. I've broken my vows and I've lied, but I didn't murder Lord Cedric's niece or her maid. The Brighton abbot drummed up these charges to protect a friend of his from investigation. He had the one witness to the crime killed. Now I'm the only thing left in the way of a smooth prosecution."

"Sariel's prosecution?" Belimai clarified.

"Yes."

"I suppose you refused to get out of the way. What am I saying? Of course you refused." Belimai shook his head. "You really are a damn saint, aren't you?"

"No, I'm not. I'm not even close. I've done mindless, stupid things." Harper closed his eyes for a moment. "I'm sorry I accused you of going back to ophorium. I should have known you never would."

"I've always kept myself so clean before." Belimai smirked. "I probably would have lost my nerve halfway to Brighton, in any case."

"No," Harper said softly, almost to himself. He knew Belimai wouldn't have. He hadn't lost his nerve when Scott-Beck had sliced him open. It had taken trained Confessors months just to get a single name from him.

"And you have the audacity to accuse me of being a martyr," Harper said.

"I shouldn't have said that." Belimai bowed his head.

"It would have come out sooner or later." Harper shrugged.

"No." Belimai reached out and touched Harper's shoulder. "I only said it to hurt you. I wanted to make you feel as bad as I did." Belimai smiled. "It's my own little way of sharing what I have with you. Aren't you lucky?"

"I think I am." Harper almost winced at his own words. He sounded like a stumbling fool. "If you had gone to the Inquisition, Belimai...I don't know what I would have done."

Harper felt suddenly horrified at how close he had just come to losing Belimai. If he hadn't woken up when he did, Belimai would have simply slipped out the door and never have come back. The thought of such a loss tore deep into Harper's chest, like a physical pain. He wanted to tell Belimai how much it hurt him. He wanted to find the words that would convey just how desperately he yearned to keep Belimai's company. All that came to his mind were the fumbled first attempts of his youth, just a string of jumbled sounds whispered into his pillow. In the intervening two decades he had taught himself to say even less. The practice of silence and evasion was no longer an effort; it was his nature. He had spent too many years distancing himself from direct honesty, and now that he wanted to find the words to make his confession, he couldn't.

Harper caught Belimai's hand gently and pulled him closer.

"Do you remember the first time we slept together?" he asked.

"Yes." Belimai frowned slightly at the change of subject. "You were so drunk I'd be surprised if you did, though."

"I remember the morning after," Harper went on. "You wanted to make sure that I didn't harbor any romantic inclination toward you. I assured you that I didn't."

"I remember." Belimai watched him intently, as if the next words Harper said might cause the floor to collapse beneath them both.

"I may have lied," Harper admitted after a moment.

The change in Belimai's expression was fractional. The corners of his mouth curved up only an increment. His thin, black eyebrows lifted just a breath. It was only the slightest smile, but there was an open, joyful honesty to it that Harper had never seen in Belimai before.

"I'm glad to hear that," Belimai replied. He dropped down on to the bed beside Harper and leaned against him. The heat of Belimai's body soaked through the chill of Harper's clothes. Harper wrapped his arms around Belimai, taking comfort in the simple sensation of holding him.

"Harper?" Belimai asked after several minutes.

"Yes?"

"What's that in the bed?" Belimai pointed to where the crushed remains of a golden pastry lay pressed between two folds of the blanket. Harper laughed. He had forgotten about the butter pastries Morris had given him. It felt like that had happened days ago.

"My breakfast. There should be another one around here somewhere."

"I see." Belimai picked the pastry up. He examined its stiff, flattened form for a moment, then took a bite.

"A little stale, but still edible." Belimai held it out to him. "Hungry?"

"I don't suppose there would be anything else to eat here, would there?" Harper asked.

"I might still have a few decayed biscuits from when I was still bothering to poison the rats."

"You're not much of one for domestic bliss, are you?" Harper took a bite out of the butter pastry. It wasn't as bad as he expected. The slightly salty flavor reminded him a little of Belimai's skin. He took another bite.

"You're hardly one to talk," Belimai replied. "I've seen your townhouse. At least I have things on the walls…Well, on the floor now, but that's not my fault. Did you just eat all of that pastry?"

"There's another one in the bed somewhere," Harper replied after swallowing the last bite.

"Fine. Leave it to me to root around in the bed, searching for bits of food." Belimai shifted through the blankets and then frowned down over the edge of the bed. "It seems to have gone missing. Hey, there's my shoe though."

"I've already eaten my fill. The shoe's all yours," Harper replied.

"Very funny." Belimai pulled the shoe out from under the bed, then sat back up beside Harper. "So what are we going to do now?" he asked.

"I don't know," Harper replied.

"Don't you?" Belimai glanced at him.

"What do you mean?"

"You know very well what I mean. It isn't like you to not have a plan in mind. I doubt that you'd even be here if you weren't planning something."

Harper kept silent.

"Harper, I almost turned myself over to the Inquisition because I didn't know what was really going on," Belimai said. "Just tell me, all right?"

"You shouldn't get involved in this," Harper said.

"I shouldn't, but I'm going to. I know myself well enough to guarantee that I won't just sit here thumbing through some cheap novel while you're being hunted down by the Inquisition. You wouldn't let me do something like that alone; why should I let you?"

Harper gazed at Belimai for several moments. His argument was absurd and exasperating, but it was also right. Had their positions been reversed, Harper would never have abandoned Belimai, not even if Belimai told him to. He wouldn't have been able to respect himself if he did such a thing. At last he sighed and stood up.

"Let's go then," he said, "I'll explain things along the way."

Belimai shot up onto his feet with a victorious smile.

"If it makes any difference," he said as he pulled on his shoes, "I lied that first morning too."

"Really?" Harper asked.

"I did know where your cap was."

Harper smiled. "I thought as much."

Chapter Twelve
Dumbwaiter

The full moon glowed behind the clouds like a paper lantern hanging in the night sky. Diffused light gleamed off the wet stones of the White Chapel walls. The rain still fell, but not heavily. Harper hardly noticed it. It had been days since he had been completely dry.

At least the miserable weather kept the guards in the back kitchen near the fire. The rain disinclined them to investigate trivial noises or notice shadowy forms moving through the haze. They hunched by the bread ovens and sipped warmed cider as Harper and Belimai crept past.

The guards could afford to be a little careless. There was only one way to break into White Chapel, and that was to climb up to the wide windows at the very top of the massive structure. The rain served the guards far better than it did any intruder. Even on a dry night, the barbed bars and sheer stone offered little climbing surface. Tonight, the wet walls glistened like glass.

Harper cursed silently as his hand skidded off a smooth corner and he began to slip. He lunged forward and grasped one of the window bars. The curving barbs of iron bit into his gloves. Harper pulled himself up before the metal tore into his hand.

Harper would have preferred to go on another night, but he didn't have time to waste. He didn't want to give Abbot Greeley a chance to find Brandson or move Lord Cedric.

He hefted himself over the iron rods to another barred window and balanced his weight on the thin lip of stone above the bars. Slowly he stretched up and groped for a hold higher up on the wall. Rain spattered against his face as he squinted up at the pale stones. He ran his gloved hands across the wet surfaces. The scabbed cut in his right palm throbbed with each motion.

At last he worked his fingers between cracks in the masonry and braced his hands.

His sore arms and back strained as he pulled himself up. A sharp pain jumped through his hand as the scab on his palm broke open. A warm gush of blood soaked through his glove and his right hand slipped. Animal panic shot through him as he swung out over the empty air of the four-story fall. He clenched his left hand desperately against the edges of stone and tried to regain his hold.

Suddenly, hot fingers grasped his right wrist. Belimai lunged down from the air and pulled Harper back against the wall. Harper felt tremors of exertion shake through Belimai's arms. Harper wedged his right foot into a crack in the stonework and pushed himself up to a thin ledge.

It was nothing more than a narrow water pipe, barely wide enough for Harper to stand on, but it held his weight. Belimai simply drifted in the air in front of him.

"You should have just let me do this. I could reach those windows easily," Belimai whispered.

"You don't know the way the building is laid out. You'd be lost once you were inside," Harper whispered back. "Did you get any of the windows open?"

"One, but it's narrow."

"I'll manage. Where is it from here?"

Belimai turned and gazed through the darkness and rain that blinded Harper. He shifted just slightly, and the air around him twisted and turned like an extension of his body, catching him as he moved. Watching him made Harper feel slightly nervous and sick. His body revolted at the mere idea of simply stepping out into the air.

Belimai turned back to Harper. "If you can follow this pipe about four feet, there's a deep crevice where a chunk of stone has come out of the mortar. That might work for a grip. The windowsill is above that."

Harper inched his way along the pipe, pressing close to the wall. Under the soft patter of the rain he could hear the minute creeks and moans as the pipe began to fold under his weight. He kept moving until, suddenly, the constant splashes of rain stopped. He looked up into the dark shadows of the overhanging windowsill.

"Can you reach the ledge?" Belimai asked from behind him.

"Not from here. The sill juts out too far," Harper said. The pipe under his left foot suddenly crumpled. Harper shifted his weight quickly, but it would only be a matter of moments before the rest of the pipe gave also.

"You're going to have to lift me up onto the sill."

"I don't think I could lift you—"

"I'll kick off from the wall to get out past the overhang. You use my momentum to push me up." Another section of the pipe folded under Harper's feet.

"This pipe's about to snap," Harper said flatly.

"I'll get you up there." Belimai moved in close behind him.

"On three." Harper drew in a deep breath. " One. Two. Three."

It took all of his will to throw himself out into the empty sky. Instinctively, his eyes squeezed shut, as if to spare him from the sight of what he had just done. His momentum pitched him out past the overhang of the windowsill. He felt Belimai's hands against the base of his back. A hard shove drove him upward. His stomach and chest slammed suddenly against a stone surface. Harper clung to it.

For a moment he simply hung there, catching his breath and calming his racing heart. Then he squeezed through the window. Belimai followed him inside.

The room was tiny and dark. Harper reached out and felt a cool surface of porcelain and then the narrow lines of water pipes. The last time he had been in White Chapel, the new flushing toilet hadn't been fully installed. Now it seemed to be up and running, though he wasn't sure how much damage he had just done to the pipes outside.

"Do you know where we are?" Belimai sounded a little out of breath from hurling him up to the window.

"In the new water-closet." Harper cracked the door and peered out into the hallway. Three gas lamps flickered on the walls, but the guards seemed to have already made their pass. The hall was empty for the moment.

"Cedric should be in the east wing. It's not too far from here." Harper had spent a long portion of the previous night and early morning watching the pale silhouettes of guards and servants in the upper rooms of White Chapel. He had seen which rooms were closed up for the evening and which received late services of wine. He had even caught a glimpse of Lord Cedric himself.

"Do you want me to follow you, or wait here?" Belimai asked.

"Neither. There's a rung ladder at the west end of this hall. It leads up to the steeple tower. They used to store festival bells and ropes up there. I need you to find the ropes. That pipe isn't going to hold for the climb back down."

"Should I meet you back here?"

He glanced back to Belimai. The tiny shaft of light that seeped in from the cracked door fell across his yellow eyes, lending them a glow. Droplets of rain glistened in his dark hair.

"No. Wait for me in the tower. You'd be a little obvious if any-one even caught a glimpse of you down in the halls. If you hear the alarms, leave the rope for me and get out."

Belimai frowned slightly at Harper's suggestion, but he didn't argue.

Harper knelt down and pulled off his wet boots. He didn't want to leave a set of muddy footprints.

"Take these with you." Harper handed Belimai his boots.

"Thanks, I'll cherish them always," Belimai replied.

"If I don't make it back, promise you'll be good to them." Harper wasn't surprised to see that the joke didn't even get a smile from Belimai.

"Be careful," Belimai told him.

"You too," Harper replied.

If they had been other people, Harper supposed, they might have said goodbye or good luck, but such exchanges held a distaste-ful trace of fatalism. Harper slipped out of the room. Behind him,

Belimai crept down the hall to the rung ladder. Harper looked back to see Belimai climb up into the shadows of the steeple tower.

Harper turned back to his own task. The distance he had to cross was no more than the length of two city blocks, but it wound through a catacomb of patrolled halls, locked doors, and up a staircase. Harper took out the keys he had stolen from Brandson.

He listened intently as he crept past the doorways, down the halls. At the sound of approaching footsteps, he unlocked one of the empty rooms and slipped inside. He waited in the dark until the noise was well out of his hearing. It was easy to elude the guards. Their hard steps and heavy boots sounded clearly against the polished stone floors. The night maids, on the other hand, were as quiet as rabbits. Only the rustling of their dresses or an occasional whisper among them gave Harper any warning of their approach.

At last he reached the east wing and the room where he had seen Lord Cedric. He leaned against the frame and listened for sounds inside. The room was quiet, but not silent. Harper made out the scratching of a pen nib against paper. There was another noise also, something Harper didn't recognize. It was a soft, hollow smacking. Or perhaps a popping. The view through the keyhole only offered a glimpse of jewel blue carpet. Harper waited, straining to discern just how many people were inside the room and what they might be doing.

The sound of writing stopped. Lord Cedric read the few lines he had written aloud. The low timbre of his voice rolled through his niece's funeral speech, and then another soft, clucking noise popped out.

Lord Cedric was absently clicking his tongue, Harper realized.

The sound of writing resumed, as did the rhythmless popping noises. Lord Cedric was unlikely to be so at ease as to slip into thoughtless habit if anyone else were in the room with him.

Harper silently unlocked the door and pulled Brandson's pistol from his pocket. Lord Cedric didn't stop writing. Only when the latch clicked closed behind Harper did Cedric glance up.

He froze in surprise at the sight of Harper. His expression was almost comical: eyes wide, lips pursed to make another pop of his tongue. The sound didn't come. He continued to stare at Harper as if he could not understand what stood before him, as if Harper were a physical impossibility.

Harper closed the distance between himself and Lord Cedric in four swift steps. He lightly rested the muzzle of Brandson's pistol against Lord Cedric's forehead. Lord Cedric's eyes managed to widen more, but his mouth remained pursed and slightly open.

"If you try to call for help, I will kill you," Harper whispered.

Lord Cedric swallowed slowly. His mouth moved, almost forming a word, but he made no sound. Harper drew the pistol back from Lord Cedric's head, allowing the man to regain a little of his composure.

"It's good that you already have your pen and ink ready. I have something for you to sign."

Harper laid out the confession that had been prepared for Sariel. It was crumpled from being in his pocket, but the Inquisition seal and watermark still stood out boldly. Lord Cedric picked up the confession, quickly skimming the tangle of legal language.

"Where it asks for the name of your accomplice in the Inquisition," Harper said, "fill in Abbot Greeley's name."

Harper watched as Lord Cedric neatly supplied the name. It gave Harper a certain pleasure to use Abbot Greeley's own weapons against him.

"Good," Harper said. "Now you sign it."

Lord Cedric dipped his pen in the inkwell, but then hesitated.

"I can offer you a great deal of money, Captain," he whispered without lifting his eyes.

"If I wanted your money, I would have asked for it. Now, sign," Harper said.

"Of course."

Lord Cedric signed the confession, then pulled his hand back as if further contact with the paper might burn him.

"I suppose it doesn't matter to you that I never intended to kill her," Lord Cedric said. "You have no idea how willful and disgraceful her behavior was. I had to—"

"You murdered her." Harper cut him off. "Then you and Abbot Greeley arranged for an innocent man to face your charges. You both deserve to hang."

"It was wrong of me. I know that. You can't know how guilty I've felt." Lord Cedric's face was a study of handsome regret. He looked nothing like Edward had when he had told Harper that he had signed a confession against him. He looked nothing like Belimai had for years after confessing Sariel's name. Lord Cedric knew so little of guilt that he couldn't even begin to approximate its self-loathing ugliness.

"My own conscience already tortures me more than you could ever wish to, Captain," Lord Cedric said softly.

"I don't want to torture you," Harper replied quietly. "I just want to see you executed."

The sad expression on Lord Cedric's face sank into an indignant glare.

"You honestly think that any judge will accept this confession, Captain? If you even get it into a court, it will be a matter of your word against mine. You don't have any witnesses, or any credibility." Lord Cedric slowly turned the plume of his pen between his fingers. "If you just let this entire matter go, I would be willing to pay you handsomely and see to it that the abbot doesn't pursue you any further. I might even be able to do something about the charges against your brother-in-law. You have to know, you don't have a chance in hell of convicting a lord. Why not let this go while you can still gain something?"

Harper picked up the confession. The ink had dried. He folded it back into his pocket and then backed to the door. He made sure the lock was secured and slid the chain lock into place.

Then he went to the window and opened it. The rain outside had gotten worse. His pulse quickened. Its fast rhythm throbbed through the cut in his palm. Harper studied the sheer wall for a moment, then turned back to study the room.

"Quite a climb, isn't it?" Lord Cedric's low voice already carried the tone of triumph.

Harper ignored Lord Cedric for the moment. He strode to the encasement for the dumbwaiter and lifted the little door. The dumbwaiter itself would be in the kitchen, many floors below. A smell of grease and seared steak drifted up from the narrow shaft. It would be tight, but he could fit down it.

Harper turned his full attention back to Lord Cedric. The other man just watched him as if he were studying the behavior of a threatening but infinitely stupid baboon. Lord Cedric seemed content in his knowledge that Harper would never succeed in bringing him to trial. He probably didn't even expect Harper to escape from White Chapel.

"I want to tell you one last thing," Harper said. "I never had any intention of laying charges against you."

"No?" Lord Cedric asked.

"I came here to see you executed." Harper raised Brandson's pistol and fired a shot directly into Lord Cedric's startled face. The silver bullet tore through Lord Cedric's skull in a gush of blood and cerebral fluid. The sound of the shot burst across the patter of falling rain with a resounding clarity.

Harper dropped Brandson's gun and swung into the dumbwaiter shaft. He had to shove with all his strength to get through the small opening. Then he dropped into an abyss. Sharp pain tore through his right hand as he shoved his arms and legs out against the walls of the shaft to slow his fall. Above him the small door fell shut, locking him into darkness. The friction of the walls burned his hands and legs.

He began to slow and, at last, stopped. Carefully he lowered himself, letting his legs take the brute effort of descending the shaft while he used his hands to feel for a door. He could hear shouts echoing from above him. The guards hadn't broken in Lord Cedric's door yet. Otherwise the alarm bells would be screaming through the entire building. He still had time, he told himself. Already the steady count had begun in the back of his thoughts. Second after second slipped past him as he groped in the darkness.

Harper's left hand brushed across the edge of a door. He gripped the narrow lip and shoved at it. The metal bit into his fingers, even through his gloves. The door was locked on the other side. Harper tried again. He shoved until his right hand crumpled. His own blood ran out from under his glove and dripped around his wrist. He wasn't going to be able to pull the lock open.

The door was thin, though. He could probably kick through it. The only problem would be the noise. Harper drew in a deep breath of the stale air around him. He needed to remain calm. Slowly, he shifted his body in the confined shaft. He rested his right leg against the little door. Between the taut line of his left leg and his back, he held himself in place against the shaft walls. The muscles of his legs and back ached, but he didn't dare to shift.

He waited for the alarms to begin their piercing screams. Then he kicked with all his strength in time with the alarms. The tin door dented and then snapped off of its hinge.

Harper pulled himself through the opening, tumbled to the floor in a dark room, and then shot to his feet. He had to reach the steeple tower before the guards organized a floor by floor search. He had already lost precious moments waiting for the alarms to sound.

He cracked the door and looked out into the hall. Three guards rushed past and turned up another hall. They were still gathering in Lord Cedric's room, Harper thought. He still had a chance. The hall was clear. Harper bolted out of the room and sprinted for the steeple tower ladder at the far end of the hall.

He vaulted up onto the iron rungs. His right hand burst with blinding pain and refused to grip. Harper shoved himself up higher and caught his weight with just his left arm. He climbed fast, pouring his fear into the furious speed of his muscles. He hardly gripped a rung before he swung his arm up for the next one. He climbed past one floor, then the next, until he bumped against the underside of the trap door.

He shoved the door aside and pulled himself up into the room. The dim glow of the shadowed moon drifted through the one tower window, illuminating the scattered forms of storage boxes and bare rafters. Harper knelt and pushed the trap door closed again.

"The guards are already searching the grounds." Harper recognized Belimai's voice, but it took him a moment to see him. He stood in a deep shadow between a huge spool of rope and the wall.

"You shouldn't still be here," Harper said between deep breaths.

"Neither should you."

"I had trouble with a door."

"Your hand looks bad." Belimai came closer.

"Does it? I can't see it very well. It feels like hell." Harper curled his left hand around the right one. His glove was slick with blood.

"You aren't going to be able to climb like that," Belimai said.

"No." Harper glanced around the room. "Help me push one of those boxes over this door."

Belimai helped him and then sat down on top of the box next to him.

"So, do you have another plan?" Belimai asked.

Harper dug through his pocket with his left hand and pulled out the confession.

"You take this to Richard Waterstone. He's the editor of the *Daily Word*. Tell him that he has to print it."

"And you?"

"I'll make a full confession against Abbot Greeley. At the very least, it will cause a scandal. It might even get charges brought up."

"They'll hang you, Harper."

"Who knows, I might get lucky—"

"Don't lie to me," Belimai snapped. "You'll be killed."

Harper wanted to come up with some other plan, but he knew there wasn't anything more he could do. At least if he were arrested, he would have a trial. His statements against Abbot Greeley would be heard and put on record. If he could get Lord Cedric's confession published at the same time, then it might spark a full investigation of the abbot's practices.

"Take the confession, Belimai," Harper said quietly.

"No. I won't—" Belimai stopped short as the noise of boots clanging against the iron rungs of the ladder drifted up from below them.

"You have to go now," Harper whispered.

"I have an idea. Come here." Belimai stood and walked to the window. Harper followed him.

Belimai pulled out his jack knife and then, before Harper could stop him, slashed the blade across his own palm.

"Belimai, what are you doing?"

Belimai thrust his bleeding hand up to Harper.

"Drink it," he said.

Harper stepped back in automatic repulsion.

"We don't have time to argue, and I'm not going to leave without you." Belimai thrust his hand out farther. Harper opened his mouth to refuse, then stopped himself. It would have been utter idiocy to refuse. He wouldn't just be dooming himself, but he would be taking Belimai with him. He lowered his head over Belimai's hand and sucked in a mouthful of blood. It was blazing hot and tasted like it had been mixed with wine. A burning trail spread across his tongue and poured down his throat as he swallowed. Heat flooded through his stomach and radiated out through his body. His muscles felt feverish and strangely fluid.

Harper drew in a breath of the cold air. The scents of gunpowder, sweat, and his own blood hung over him. He could also smell Belimai's hair and the rats lurking in the dark corners of the room.

There was a loud crack as one of the guards rammed against the blocked trap door.

Harper took another swallow of the blood that pooled up from Belimai's hand. He concentrated on the wind pouring in from the open window. The currents of air and falling rain swung and turned like solid masses. He reached out and touched a gust of wind. It rolled under his fingers and shifted as he turned his hand.

"Can you feel it?" Belimai asked.

"Yes." Despite the urgency, Harper couldn't help but feel amazed. The dark hollow of the night transformed around him.

Rich tones of violet and blue tinted the currents of wind. They rolled over Harper, touching his burning skin and brushing through his hair like curious fingers. Droplets of rain and pungent scents hung on the winds like thousands of brilliant beads.

Another loud crack rang through the small room. This time it was the sound of the wooden trap door splintering under the blow of an ax. The box on top of the door jarred with the impact.

"We have to go." Belimai jumped up onto the window frame and then dived out.

Harper climbed up after him. He crouched on the sill for a long moment, assuring himself that he wasn't about to throw himself to his death. The wind wrapped around him and pulled at his arms. Belimai looked back at him from the midst of the swirling air. Harper took a deep breath and stepped out into the open arms of the night.

He fell for an instant. Then suddenly, a rush of wind swept up from beneath him and lifted him high up into the sky. The air rolled under him and rose like a cresting wave. He turned and twisted like the drops of rain caught in the wind with him. Each shift of his hands or twist of his body swung him out in another direction. He soared from one rushing current to the next without knowing how to control his flight.

In a matter of moments he was blown far out over the city steeples and smoking chimneys. Rising gusts from the river swept up and gently lifted him higher into the sky. The searchlights at White Chapel glittered like distant stars. The waters of the river below him moved like the glossy body of a small centipede. A thrill of both fear and exhilaration shivered through Harper's stomach. Harper closed his eyes, concentrating on moving his body through the columns of tumbling air.

He felt Belimai's hand close around his wrist. Harper glanced over to see Belimai holding his hand and soaring beside him. He relaxed and moved with Belimai, emulating the small turns and twists Belimai used to glide between the currents. As he moved with Belimai, some instinct deep in his blood seemed to awaken. A natural sense of how to manipulate the swelling waves of the wind flowed through him.

He turned and floated slowly back toward the glimmering lights of the city.

"Where to now?" Belimai asked.

"To see Richard Waterstone. We need to deliver his headline news to him." Harper felt a giddy grin spreading across his face. Ribbons of wind tickled his outstretched arms. He laughed. He should have been in pain and exhausted, but at that precise moment, he felt as if nothing could ever be wrong in his life.

Belimai glanced at him and laughed back.

"Why so happy suddenly?" Belimai asked.

"I just realized what a beautiful night it was." Harper pulled closer to Belimai and kissed him.

Epilogue
Solitaire

A deep red glow soaked through the curtains and filled the room as the sun slowly sank into the embrace of evening. I flipped through a deck of cards, carefully marking the aces. There wasn't much else to do. I had been waiting for well over two hours, attempting to maintain the appearance of ease. I propped my legs up on a chair and purposefully slouched a little more.

There was a sound of footsteps on the stairs, then the scent of soap and leather. The door opened quietly and Harper came in. He placed his cap on the rack and then hung up his heavy coat. He looked tired, as always.

"Oh, it's you, is it?" I asked.

"I haven't been gone so long that you've forgotten about me, have I?" he asked.

"How could I? You've been in the papers every day." I set the cards aside. "From the last I read I would suppose congratulations are in order," I said.

"You'd suppose?" Harper peeled off his gloves and tossed them across the pile of newspapers on the table in front of me.

"Papers have been known to get their stories wrong," I said.

"Yes, I'll give you that." Harper dropped down into the seat across from mine. He lit a cigarette and took in a deep breath of the smoke. The weakness of his right hand was hardly perceptible anymore. Only the thick, red scar remained as evidence of how badly hurt and infected the flesh had been.

"They misspelled your middle name, by the way," I told him.

"Did they?" Harper squinted at the litter of pages. "Jubaal. At least it wasn't Judas. I don't even care. I'm just glad to have the court proceedings and hearings done with."

"So, it's over?"

"It's done. I went to the gallows myself this afternoon to be sure," Harper said. "The abbot is most certainly dead and done with."

According to the papers, Abbot Greeley had ordered Captain Brandson to assassinate Lord Cedric to suppress a confession that Cedric had signed. Apparently, it had implicated them both in the murder of Lord Cedric's niece. The story in the papers made Lord Cedric out to be a kind man brought low by one moment of rage and terrible misfortune. Abbot Greeley, on the other hand, had taken on a deeply sinister role. There was even an implication that the abbot had been using the niece's death to blackmail Lord Cedric.

It was a remarkable work a fiction that Harper had strung together with confessions and tiny pieces of evidence. Brandson's pistol, left at the scene of Lord Cedric's murder, struck me as a particularly nice detail.

If he had wanted, Harper could have indulged in a little gloating or self-congratulation. He had certainly worked things out well enough to deserve it. Instead, he was quiet and thoughtful. He was acting as if there were something he still had to attend to. I shuffled through my deck of cards to give myself something to do.

The papers had mentioned other things, but I waited for Harper to bring them up.

"A game of cards?" I asked.

"Not yet. It's nice to just sit here and do nothing."

"It's not all that easy, you know. I've been sitting around trying to do nothing for the last two weeks."

"Your rooms look good," Harper said. "Did you paint the walls white?"

"No. I just washed them."

"Hmm." Harper wasn't paying much attention to the conversation. I knew him well enough to recognize the times when he was working his way to an unpleasant subject. I absently dealt myself a hand a solitaire. Harper smoked in silence for a while.

"I was surprised at how many people came out to see him swing," Harper said. "I don't think he even saw me in the crowd."

I didn't know quite how to respond. The abbot's destruction had been Harper's passion for the last month. He had been at the courthouse for days on end, giving testimony and presenting evidence. All that he had seemed to want was the abbot's public execution. Now he had it. The abbot had not been punished for any one of his real crimes. None of the harm he had done had been undone. All the execution had given Harper was revenge. I wondered if that had been enough for him.

"You could put a queen there," Harper suggested as I turned the cards through my hands.

I nodded and laid the card down.

Steadily I slid card after card into the long columns of suits and numbers. At last I had only two cards left, and neither of them could be placed.

"You could trade them for others in the deck," Harper offered.

"Advising me to cheat against myself, Captain?"

"I'm told it's common practice." He took a last drag of his cigarette and then crushed it out against the newspaper. The smell of singed newsprint and tobacco curled through the air.

"I don't feel like it today." I folded the two cards and set them down.

"Was that a bottle of wine I noticed when I came in?" Harper asked as I shuffled the cards back into a single deck.

"The finest from Hells Below," I said. "Would you like some?"

"I believe I would." Harper smiled briefly. He looked good smiling. It brushed away the fine lines of exhaustion and overwork that had become etched into the corners of his eyes.

I got up, opened the bottle, and handed it to Harper.

"No glass?" he asked.

"They were all smashed. I still haven't gotten any new ones. How about a bowl?" I offered, thinking it might amuse him.

"The bottle's fine."

I sat back down and watched Harper carefully lift the bottle with his left hand. The motion looked surprisingly natural. He pushed the bottle aside after he had taken a long drink.

"Did you find Edward?" he asked.

"Yes. He's fine. So is your sister."

"They still haven't run into each other?"

"They have." I shoved the cork back into the neck of the wine bottle to stop its thick odor from crawling out into the room.

"And?" Harper prompted.

"And your brother-in-law has to be some kind of saint. He's started working with Good Commons. Your sister and he seem to have patched things up. They're both doing quite well."

"That's good." Harper nodded.

"The wine is from Sariel. A token of his thanks."

Harper nodded and I continued shuffling my cards. Harper leaned back in his chair and closed his eyes. I played another game of solitaire and left him alone. Sooner or later he would tell me what I already knew from reading through the papers. I could have cut him short and brought it up myself, but there was no point. I was as willing as he was to let it wait.

I enjoyed simply sitting with him. It felt easy and comfortable.

"Belimai," he said at last.

"Yes?" I glanced over to him. His eyes were still closed, his head tilted slightly as if he were almost falling asleep.

"Did the paper say anything else about me?"

"Aside from how courageously you served the cause of Justice, and what a nice profile you had?"

"Yes, aside from that." Harper's voice was serious, but his body remained limp in the chair.

"It mentioned that you might be offered a position as an abbot, possibly at the Covenant Inquisition House." I looked down at my cards.

"I have."

"Oh. Well, congratulations again." I stopped playing with the cards. Covenant Abbey was far from Hells Below and far from me. Harper could hardly be abbot there and still be seen in my company, or the company of any Prodigal.

I realized that the last business Harper had to deal with would be me.

"So, when will you be going?" I asked.

"I didn't accept it," Harper said.

"You didn't?"

I was so prepared for another answer that it took me a moment to understand what I had heard.

"No, I tendered my resignation."

"You what?"

"I resigned." Harper opened his eyes and looked at me. "I'm as done with the Inquisition as Abbot Greeley is."

"Why?" I stared at Harper. He didn't say anything. For several moments he continued gazing at me, then turned and uncorked the wine bottle. He took another deep drink, then picked up the cork with his right hand and carefully pushed it back into the bottle.

"If you don't want to tell me, then never mind," I told him as the silence began to stretch on. I dealt myself another hand of cards. They were a worthless mix of deuces, jacks, and fours. I scowled at the cards and then folded them down onto the tabletop.

"You know Brandson didn't hire on to a ship and escape, don't you?" Harper said.

"I just assumed you killed him. Why?" I asked.

Harper glanced down at his scarred palm and then looked at the wine bottle. After a moment he shifted his attention back to me.

"Does it bother you that I killed two men and falsified evidence, just to see Abbot Greeley publicly executed? Just to satisfy my need for revenge?"

It didn't bother me in the least, but I could see that it did disturb Harper.

"The abbot had committed more than enough crimes to deserve what he got. I think the same could be said for Lord Cedric and Captain Brandson. We both know that there was no other way they would be punished," I told Harper.

"Brandson was just an idiot." Harper sipped a little more wine.

"Harper," I said, "he deserved it. I can't believe you think he didn't."

"I know he deserved it," Harper replied calmly.

"Then what is this all about?" I demanded.

Harper smiled slightly.

"I'm telling you why I resigned," he said.

"Oh." I shuffled the cards again. "So, why?"

"I knew Abbot Greeley had been protecting Lord Cedric because the man was a friend of his, but it never struck me until today that I might have done the same thing. It was the same with Scott-Beck. Abbot Greeley protected and helped him because the man was a friend of his."

"He was a bastard. They all were," I said. It was still too easy to remember Scott-Beck's pleased face as he leaned over me, cutting my body open.

"Yes, but they thought they were right in doing what they did—"

"They weren't," I stated flatly.

"Let me finish, will you?" Harper asked.

"All right, fine. Go on. They thought they were right..."

"Just like I believe I am right—"

"But you are right," I put in quickly.

"Belimai."

"Fine, go on. I won't interrupt anymore." I leaned back in the chair and crossed my arms over my chest.

"All I'm saying is that I realized that I had the same potential to willfully break the law that the abbot did." Harper took a quick drink of wine. "Let's face it, Belimai: I'm not much of a priest to begin with, and when it comes to being an Inquisitor...Well, the letter of the law isn't my strong point. If I became an abbot, that wouldn't change. In my own way, I'd be as bad as Abbot Greeley."

"So you resigned?" I asked.

"I turned down the position as abbot because of that. I resigned because I just don't want to do this anymore. I'm tired of it." Harper shook his head.

"So, what now?" I asked

"Now? I just want to be happy. I want to enjoy my life."

"To be happy," I said suspiciously. It was such a deceptively simple-sounding thing to say. It could mean anything. "How do you plan on being happy?"

"How do you?" Harper returned the question.

"I'm not the sort to make plans," I said. "You are."

"True," Harper admitted.

"So, what is this plan of yours?" I picked up my discarded hand of cards. They were as hopeless as ever, but it gave me something to do.

"I'm going back to the Foster Estate. It's mine, and it's about time I took care of it."

"So, the simple life of a rural landlord for you, then?" I gave up on the cards I had and pulled three new ones from the deck. Harper was free to go as he pleased. He was free to find his happiness wherever he wished. I smacked my hand of cards back down next to the deck in frustration.

"Wouldn't you want to get away from here if you could?" Harper asked.

"What, and leave all the smog and Inquisitors behind?" Of course I wanted to leave. Every Prodigal I knew wanted to get away from the city, but there were laws and guards to stop us.

"You'd be leaving your home, your friends—everything," Harper said. "I know it's a hard thing for me to ask you to do. But I have to ask."

"You're serious?" I stared at Harper. "You want me to come with you?"

"You wouldn't leave the bell tower at White Chapel without me," Harper said. "Why should I leave you here?"

"That was hardly the same thing," I said.

"We can leave tonight while my name is still on the active lists of Inquisitors. All we need to do is trade coats. The clerks at the Green-Hill carriage house already think you're me."

"Harper, what if we get out to your estate and we..."

"We're found out? We're attacked by locusts?" Harper shrugged. "Who knows what will happen, but I want to find out. Don't you, Belimai?"

"What if we find out that we can't stand each other?" I asked.

"It's a big house. I'm sure we could work something out."

"I'm serious," I said.

"You're too serious." Harper pulled off his Inquisition jacket and tossed it at me.

"People are going to know—" I told him.

"Not if we're careful."

"It's not that simple, Harper."

"It is. Just come with me."

I stared at him, trying to think of what I would do if I chose not to join him. I wasn't such a delicate creature that I would simply wither and die of sorrow. I could survive losing him; I just wouldn't want to.

At last, I pulled on the jacket. It was still warm from Harper's body, and the familiar scent of his skin lingered on it. I buttoned the front and straightened the collar. It fit me well enough.

ACKNOWLEDGMENTS

I would like to thank Nicole Kimberling and Melissa Miller for all their support, nagging and patience. I'm also grateful to Marjorie M. Liu who was kind enough to read an early draft and who offered amazing encouragement.

And, of course, I have to thank Sharon McMorrow who taught me that literature could contain spicy sex scenes as well as proper grammar.